I Love You, Always, Forever

By

Charlie Dean

Cover design by
Charlie Dean

For Natalie

Chapter 1

Pulling up to my old childhood home on a wet Monday morning was not the way I'd envisioned this week starting. I should have been in Majorca now, sitting under the shade of a palm tree, sand beneath my toes and slowly but surely drinking my way through every cocktail on the menu of the beach bar.

But here I was, driving down the tree-lined avenue where I played as a child, friends long since moved on. Some of the old neighbours were still there. There's Paul and Joe who can finally be openly gay even though they've been a couple since the mid-seventies grabbing shopping from the car and getting in out of the rain as quickly as possible.

Mrs Tanner, the nosey neighbour who knows everyone's business and takes great pleasure in telling anyone who will listen is as usual standing at the window. I'm actually thankful of the rain now, because otherwise she'd be outside like a shot ready to chew my ear off and I'm just not in the mood for idle gossip today.

The avenue still looks the same to me, even now, with my forty-six-year-old eyes.

And it always feels like stepping back in time, a time of innocence where I had nothing and no one to worry about. Days spent with my friends at school or in the park. Where summer seemed to last forever, and Christmas was indeed the most wonderful time of the year.

But today, I wanted to be anywhere but here. I wanted to be far, far away from this day. It is a day that could change my life in every possible way. A day, no one ever wants to go through.

Pulling up on the drive always feels like coming home even though I moved out over twenty years ago, I never refer to it as my parents' home. It's just home. Just like the house I live in now is home. I've only ever lived in two places my entire life and they are both home. Both have people in them that are my family, my blood and both are places I feel safe in. But this house, where I grew up, is something more than that.

Time seems to stand still whenever I visit. It echoes with childhood memories of me and my brother growing up. There sit my grandparents on the chairs we've borrowed from next door for Mum's annual New Year's Eve party, even though they never stay till New Year and Dad always had to drive them home around ten o' clock.

There's where I used to make fort tents and sit and read for hours under the table. The back window ledge that I used as a desk to play teachers and the soft carpet I used to lie on watching Byker Grove whilst doing my homework and crushing on Declan Donnelly

'How on earth can you do your homework like that?' Mum always asked.

'It's just comfy.' I would reply whilst working out an algebra equation set by Mr Patel or working on a story for Mr Royston. 'And the day one of my teachers tells you I haven't been doing my homework or that my grades are falling, then that's the day you can tell me to sit at the table.' Sounds a little bit sassy now I come to think of it. And eventually, during A Levels, I moved to the dining room table. Essays on the Russian Revolution using textbooks was a lot easier with a table made for eight to spread everything out on.

However, today isn't the day for a trip down memory lane. Today doesn't involve happy conversations and chats over a cup of tea. Reminiscing about family holidays and flicking through photo albums. No, today is a far more serious day.

Turning off the engine, I unplug my phone from the auxiliary port where Depeche Mode and Tori Amos have kept me company on the journey here. I only live a few miles away, but the journey still takes twenty minutes, thirty if you don't catch the lights or get caught behind a tractor on the country roads where I live.

There are three messages in my friends' WhatsApp group all wishing me luck for today, fingers crossed that all goes well, you know the kind of thing. I smile at their good wishes and remember a time when we worried about nothing but homework, making up stories and playing Uno during lunch outside the sixth form block so we could ogle the cute older boys.

But time has moved on. We see each other as much as we can. Claire moved down to London and has a high-flying career in recruitment. India and Lyn married a few years after me, settled down and had children. All three of us work and keep house and bring up the children. Honestly, sometimes I think the feminist movement did us seventies kids an injustice. We're expected to be housewives, mothers and to keep a job as well.

Then I look at my daughter, flying high at university, the first in our family to do so. Newly engaged to a man who sees her as an equal, loves her unquestionably and treats her with love and respect. And that's when I know that it's all been worth it. She has opportunities now that I never had. And yes, it's still not entirely equal in the world, but it's getting there and maybe, by the time she has children of her own, they will be the first truly equal generation.

Just arrived. I write in the chat and then pop my phone away in my bag. I can hear the rain pounding on the roof of the car, see it streaming down the windows and I think to myself that I'll just stay inside, lock myself away from what is before me. But I know that I can't and with a huge mental effort, I fling open the door, close it as quickly as possible and dash to the front door.

'Anyone could walk in here.' I say my usual greeting even though I've used the key. But no one replies. The house is in darkness, just as I left it last time. The curtains are closed at the front and due to the dreariness of the day, hardly any light is filtering through from the back either. The dreariness matches my mood though and I'm loathed to open the curtains and let in any amount of light. Why should I? I don't feel in any way light-hearted.

It's then that I catch sight of my parents' wedding photo, the one I had mounted into a frame years ago with my grandparents' wedding photos on either side. It's then that I see these smiling faces, long since passed, and I know they are with me, here in spirit rather than flesh. That their blood flows in my blood and they would not want me to be sad or scared.

Chin up. I hear them say and I pull the curtains back with a determination that I did not feel before. A determination to face whatever the day holds and to meet it head on like the Deans have always done. To remain steadfast in the knowledge that whatever the news, it will be dealt with and handled in the appropriate manner.

Tea is definitely needed so I head into the kitchen, flick on the kettle and open the cupboard, taking out my dad's mug, mine now and smile again at the two child size cups that Mum has kept all these years. Mugs that were used for hot blackcurrant drinks in winter. I then spot Nan's pink jug she used to make honey and lemon when we were ill and ice-cold milk during summer and I can almost feel her presence beside me conjuring up said delicacies.

Memories hang around the rooms like ghosts and I swear, if I concentrate hard enough, I can hear the four of us laughing at Blackadder, playing Monopoly on Christmas Day or my dad snoring as he fell asleep after a long day at work.

I leave the tea bag in the hot water to mash for a few minutes and head upstairs. Although it's all been redecorated many times since I left, it still feels the same. The stairs are steep and narrow, something I never noticed as a child. My box room sits at the front, my toys neatly arranged on the bed. And there he is. Brown Ted.

Threadbare on his chest from the constant cuddling, he's looking a bit limper now due to a loss of stuffing after a minor accident with our dog Sully. However, he's still my Brown Ted.

Sitting down on the bed, I hold him to my chest. My anxiety slips away for a moment, just like the nightmares of my youth when a kiss from Mum or Dad and a hug from Brown Ted was enough to soothe me back to sleep.

A loud knock on the door startles me slightly. It will be my brother, although why he's knocking, I'm not sure. I peek out of the window and it's Joe from up the road. He'll have seen my car and come to ask questions I'm not ready to answer, so I duck down on the floor.

And then I see it.

Oh, the memories that lie within.

I reach under my bed and pull out the wooden box my dad made me to keep my treasures in. There's a sun and moon carved on top; it matched my bedroom at the time, and I run my hands over the smooth design that took my dad and I hours to sand until it was just right.

Lifting the lid feels like opening a time machine.

Old school reports, newspaper cuttings, sports day medals. Holiday souvenirs, keepsakes, and photos. And there, underneath it all, are my diaries.

They haven't been opened in years; I think the last time I looked at them was when my children were little. I lean up against my bed, knees bent, and reach for the earliest one I can see, 1990. This is the year I turned fourteen and my third year at senior school.

I rest the green book on my knees and turn the first page. At first, I'm taken aback by my neat and tidy writing, but then I remember that I always tried to write with my finest handwriting to begin with, and, as I flick through the pages my typical, scruffy scrawl returns halfway through January.

A lot of the pages are blank. I wasn't a very good diarist to start off with. I wrote general rubbish about what I'd done that day, moans about how much homework we'd been given but then, as I'm flicking through, August seems rather bulky, in fact, August has extra pages of writing stuck to the original pages.

My mind draws a blank as to what happened, my menopausal memory failing me as usual, so I eagerly turn to the month of August and as I begin to read it, I remember. August the 17th, 1990 was my first kiss.

Chapter 2

'For the last time, Charlotte!' I can hear the exasperation in Mum's voice, but I'm having far too much fun to care. 'Don't make me come in there and get you!' she warns, but I know it's an idle threat. Mum doesn't do pools or the sea or water of any kind. In fact, Mum sits by the pool or on the beach soaking up the rays and enjoying a good book.

After all, it is her holiday as well. She looks after me and my older brother, cleans the house, does the shopping, cooks all the meals for fifty weeks of the year so for the two weeks that we come on holiday she gets to chill for a bit while Dad looks after us, well just me now.

My older brother Rob is at home. He's almost nineteen, has a full-time job and didn't want to come. It's the first time he's been left alone in the house for this amount of time, so naturally we make the trip to the public phone at camp reception three times a day to check he's alive and hasn't as yet burnt the house down.

My mum's parents live next door, so it's not like he's really on his own, anyway. Grandad has been charged with making sure he leaves for work on time and locks the door behind him and Nan cooks him tea every day. So, it's almost like we're still at home to be fair.

'Charlotte Anne Dean!' There it is, my full name, only to be used in times of extreme naughtiness. 'Get out of the pool this minute.' I can see Mum is getting a little embarrassed now, but there's hardly anyone left by this time. It's a well-known fact that you have to be out of the pool, showered and eaten tea so you can grab a table in the club for the evening's entertainment. Woe betide if you turn up after seven and expect a seat, if you're late, it's tough luck, you're standing up for the duration, hovering around like a hawk waiting for someone to leave so you can swoop in. 'I'll get your father!' This is the other warning sign that I've pushed it too far.

'One more go please?' I beg and she reluctantly gives in.

'One more, then out and back to the caravan.' She wags a finger at me. 'Your towel and flip flops are here.' She points to a sun bed and then heads off back to our caravan.

'Yes!' I leap out of the pool and run up the steps that lead to the flume. We've been coming to Littlesea in Weymouth for years. The same two weeks, the same campsite over and over again, but it never gets boring. When I reach the top, I can see for miles. I shiver slightly at the sea breeze that I can feel on my wet skin. There's a boy in front of me, about my age, just standing there. 'Are you going?' I ask.

'In a minute.' He's looking at something in the distance.

'What you looking at?' I follow his gaze towards the caravans.

'My mum said she'd wave from the window when dinner was ready.' He shrugs his shoulders and then sits down at the top of the water slide. 'Ah well, one more go.' He pushes himself off and flies down the slide. I follow a few seconds later. There isn't a lifeguard, so you just counted to ten and hoped the other person didn't get stuck on the way down. Unfortunately, this time, the other person had gotten stuck. 'Oi!'

'Sorry.' I say as my feet bashed into his back. 'The water seems to have stopped.'

'I can see that Dumbo.' He looks over his shoulder at me. 'Get your feet off me.' He pushes my feet with his hands.

'Don't call me Dumbo. It's not my fault, is it?' We sit there for what felt like hours, but it was only a few seconds before the water started running again. The boy pushes himself away, sticking out his tongue as he went. 'Boys!' I shake my head, holding myself back for a few seconds to allow him time to get out of the way.

Even though I was expecting it, the splash into the pool comes with a shock of cold water and the slight panic when you fully submerge before kicking your way to the top. I took a deep breath as I broke the surface, but it was a little too early and I inhaled a mouthful of water and began choking.

'You ok?' The boy was by my side at once, gently slapping my back. 'It's ok, you're safe.' We wade to the side of the pool and hitched ourselves out, sitting on the edge, our feet dangling in the water. 'I'm Joey, by the way.' He holds out his hand and I shake it as firmly as I could, bearing in mind both of us were very wet.

'Charlie.' I say quickly off the top of my head. No one ever called me Charlie. I had previously begged my parents to call me Charlie, but they had point blank refused, saying it was a boy's name and so Charlotte I had remained. Grandpa Dean had called me Lottie once to which my mum had frowned, pursed her lips at him in the way only she can do, and he'd never done it since. 'Charlotte really, but my mum doesn't like Charlie.'

'I'm Joseph really, named after my Grandad, but I like Joey, it's much cooler.' He kicks his feet in the pool, making a huge splash. 'I'll call you Charlie if you want.'

'Thanks.' I splash my feet in time with his, enjoying our new companionship. 'When did you get here?' I took in his pale white skin compared to mine that was now developing a deep tan due to a week of being constantly exposed to the sun.

'Just this morning.' I nod. 'You?'

'Been here for a week.' I say smugly. 'Where are you from?' I couldn't detect an accent, but then I wasn't very good at accents unless they were something like French or Scottish. I stood up and headed towards the sun bed and wrapped my towel around me before slipping my feet into my flip-flops.

'Kent.' He smiles. 'You're from Coventry, aren't you?' He asks.

I looked at him in astonishment. 'How did you know that?'

'Magic.' He whispers, then laughs. 'Not really, you've got Coventry City Football Club on your towel.'

'It's my brother's.' I secretly thanked my mum for bringing this one and not my Care Bear's one. Although I loved it, it was a little childish for a fourteen-year-old to have a Care

Bear towel. 'I'd best get back.' I was suddenly reluctant to leave and noticed Joey's face seemed downcast too.

'I can walk with you if you want.' I nodded eagerly and felt a little flip in my stomach when he smiled at me.

'Haven't you got a towel?' He shakes his head.

'Nah.' We walk between the sun beds. 'My dad's doing a BBQ, so we'll be sitting outside anyway.'

We walked and chatted, weaving our way through row upon row of perfectly symmetrical caravans, most having a car parked outside. Some had windbreaks set up and outdoor furniture. As we walked, we could hear mums shouting at children to stop messing about, dads chatting outside as they lit BBQs and children playing football or tennis. One family even had a paddling pool set up.

'This is me.' We'd reached my caravan, the door wide open and Dad's Morris Marina taking pride of place beside it.

'Really?' Joey sounds surprised. 'I'm just there.' He points to the caravan opposite. 'How cool is that?' He starts to walk off.

'Are you going to the club later?' I ask quickly.

'Of course.' And with that, he was gone, giving me a quick wave as he disappeared around the front of his caravan.

'What are you doing loitering about?' Dad asks as he stepped outside the door dressed in his blue jeans, shirtless but wearing socks and Jesus sandals. I love my dad, but his sense of style is somewhat lacking. 'Your dinner is on the table and your mum just popped in the shower. I'm off to check on your brother, so be a good girl and eat it all up.' He heads off towards reception. 'And there's jelly in the fridge and squirty cream.'

Jelly and cream. My mouth waters at the thought but then I remember there's a full roast dinner to eat beforehand. Even on holiday, unless we've had fish and chips or gone to the pub, Mum insists on cooking huge meals.

You still need your meat and vegetables. She would insist, even though the temperature here in Weymouth was usually around thirty degrees, and the last thing you wanted to do was eat roasted chicken and hot gravy.

I can hear the shower running and my mum singing Cliff Richard songs, so I decide to eat outside for a change. We don't have a table and chairs outside, we've rented off Haven, but Dad always packs some folding garden chairs so I plonk myself down and tuck in.

'Pssst!' I look up to see Joey's face peeking around the front of his caravan. 'Fancy a burger?' I want nothing more than to say yes but I know Mum will go berserk, so I shake my head and show him my plate. He mimes throwing up, placing his hand on his stomach and doubling over, pretending to wretch. I giggle at once.

'Is that you, Charlotte?' It's Mum.

'Yes, Mum.' I call. Joey looks slightly guilty and disappears again.

'Are you eating your dinner?'

'Of course, Mum.' I put a piece of chicken in my mouth, even smothered in gravy, it's dry and tasteless. Mum is usually a fantastic cook, but when it comes to chicken, she's so worried that she'll give us salmonella that the chicken is always cooked within an inch of its life.

'Well, make sure you eat it all, then put your plate in the bowl and come get in the shower. I've laid your pink dress out for you.' I roll my eyes. One day, I'll be able to choose my own outfits.

'Can't I wear my black bolero jacket and Ra Ra skirt?' I had this cute outfit for Christmas and it makes me feel like Janet Jackson.

'You wear far too much black these days.' She's right, I do. It's something I'm finding myself more and more comfortable with. It doesn't show sweat, a huge plus point since I've hit puberty. It makes me feel slimmer, another plus point since I've put on three stone since turning eleven and I can be invisible in black.

'Is that a yes, then?' I can hear the hairdryer now so I assume that's her answer and gobble my dinner, skip pudding and get myself ready before she can change her mind. By the time I step out of the bedroom, we're already running late because there was a huge queue for the phone and my brother decided to be out. Mum eyes me up and down and does the lip pursing thing before looking at her watch and flapping that all the good tables will be taken.

A small victory but a victory none the less.

Chapter 3

As usual, the club is packed full of families. Gone are the days when parents left the children in the chalet to sleep, and staff walked round the site checking and announcing, 'baby crying in chalet 60' and a rather squiffy mother would have to head back. Now, holidays are for the kids just as much as the parents.

When we arrived, Mum's eagle eye spotted a table right in the middle. I watched her skills as she quickly navigated through the throng of people and saw the disappointed look on the family who headed to the bar first. Rookie error. Mum gets the table and dad gets the drinks. That's the way it works.

I've got my bottle of pop, a straw obviously and a packet of ready salted crisps. Dad has, of course, complained about the prices. 'I could buy ten of these in the shop' and Mum has finally relaxed with a large glass of white wine.

Bingo is always first, and I always fidget. I find it so difficult to sit still and quiet when I have to, even though I have a book with me. It's the same old story though, when you have to do something, you can't. I can sit still reading at home for hours, but once you tell me that's what I must do…well…it just becomes impossible. Mum has looked at me no less than three times in five minutes and an elderly lady at the next table has tutted twice when I giggled out loud.

The Sweet Valley High series is my current read. I'm desperate to read Judy Blume's Forever after Claire told me they had sex in it but when I asked my mum to get me a copy, she said she'd heard about it from one of the mum's at school and I wasn't to read it. Claire said she'd lend me her copy when she gets it back from her cousin. Claire's mum is so much cooler than mine.

Finally, bingo ends and after a short interval of handing out prizes, the cabaret comes on.

'Can I go to the arcade, please?' This is my cue to head off. Mum hands me a bag of pennies that she saves over the whole year. Split into fourteen equal bags. I've learnt to make them last and not ask for anymore although, usually after a pint or two, Dad will slip me another fifty pence.

The arcade is full of children, some my age, lots slightly younger and older teenagers trying to look cool with their younger siblings attached to their legs. This is the curse of being the eldest. You have the privilege of looking after your brothers and sisters. I can see one girl, about sixteen maybe, with full makeup and large hair probably spritzed with a full can of hairspray, trying to talk to a boy about the same age. She's curling a strand of hair round her finger and making puppy dog eyes at him, but his little brother keeps tugging at his shirt.

The penny shove machine is where I'm heading, though. I walk around it, looking for a space with some coins dangling over the edge.

'That looks like a good one.' I turn to see Joey standing behind me. His brown hair is very tidily styled now, and he's wearing a white t-shirt and blue jeans. He's even got Nike trainers on. What I wouldn't give for a pair of Nike trainers.

'Do you think there's enough on the back shelf though?' I ask, trying to ignore the funny feeling going on in my stomach as Joey leans over me to have a closer look. He smells lovely, Lynx Oriental. My brother got a set for Christmas and covers himself in it for Saturday nights at Mr G's nightclub.

'I reckon so.' He leans on the machine by the side of me.

'Here we go.' I've only used a few pennies and already the machine has dropped more than I've put in.

'Told you.' He says with a grin on his face. 'Do you want a slush?'

'I haven't got any money.' This isn't strictly true. I do have money, holiday money that my grandparents gave me before we left, but I'm saving it to buy some souvenirs and presents for everyone. You can't go on holiday without bringing back presents.

'It's ok.' He pulls out a ten-pound note from his back pocket and my mouth falls open in shock. 'Dad gave me this earlier.'

'But you'll need it for the rest of your holiday.' I had naturally assumed it was his whole spend for the week.

'He'll give me another one tomorrow.' Joey shrugs. 'Coming?' I grab the pennies from the machine and pop them safely in the little black shoulder bag I got for my birthday. 'Red, blue or mixed?' he asks.

'Mixed please.' I never understood why the strawberry flavour was red and raspberry blue. I mean, who said strawberries were more important than raspberries or was strawberry flavour easier to make and so came first?

We head out of the arcade and over to the pool. It's just getting dark, and the lights are flickering. The slush is freezing in my hands but it's a welcome relief as it's quite humid away from the sea. We sit down next to each other on a sunbed, and I make the fatal error of drinking too quickly and giving myself a brain freeze.

'What do you want to be when you grow up?' Joey asks a few minutes later when my brain has returned to normal.

'I'd like to be a writer.' It's a dream of mine to write stories.

'What? Books and stuff?' he asks and I nod. 'Do you like books?'

'Yeah.' I'm not about to tell him how much, though, he might think I'm a nerd. 'You?'

'Not really.' He bashes the ice in his slush. 'I'm more into football and Nintendo.'

'Have you got a Nintendo?' Rob was currently saving up to buy one.

'Haven't you?' he asks, and I shake my head. 'They're brilliant. Dad got it for me. He's a surgeon, you know. That's what I'm going to be when I'm older.' He sounded like he was bragging a little, maybe trying to impress me, I thought. It's all boys seem to try to do these days.

'Have you got any brothers or sisters?' I've already sucked the juice out of my slush and it's now just ice, so I place it on the floor.

'Two older sisters, much older.' He rolls his eyes. 'They're in their twenties and all about getting married and having babies. Honestly, it's all they talk about.'

'Don't you want to get married one day?' I'm currently trying to stop the vision of me walking down the aisle in a white dress.

'Yeah, but not till I'm old.' He replies. 'You know, about thirty.'

'I want to get married at twenty-three and have my first baby at twenty-four.' Don't ask me why I wanted this.

'You sound just like Becky.' He rolls his eyes again. 'She's been going out with this lad for two years now and she's convinced he's going to propose anytime soon.'

'It's kind of what girls do,' I say. 'Except for my friend Claire. She said she'd never get married and never have children.'

'Girls go all weird when you mention love and stuff.' His slush is now pure ice as well, and he puts it next to mine on the floor and leans back on his arms. 'Look at us. We're just two mates sitting by the pool having a drink. Tomorrow we'll probably have a laugh in the pool together.' He turns his head to look at me. 'You are going to the pool tomorrow, aren't you?'

'I think so.' It was generally what we did every day. We'd head out somewhere in the morning and then sit by the pool in the afternoon.

'I'll meet you here tomorrow then. It can be our spot.'

And that's how the next week went. Afternoons were spent in the pool and flume with Joey. His parents had even started sitting next to mine. They'd save each other seats in the club, buy each other rounds of drinks, and then Joey and I would head out to the arcade. One of the evenings we were even invited to Joey's caravan after the club, and we played cards while our parents sat drinking and laughing.

Then all too soon it was Friday night, my family's last night.

'Will you write to me?' I ask Joey as we sit in our spot by the pool.

'Yeah, of course I will.' He smiles at me. 'Won't be the same here without you.'

'Perhaps you'll come here next year too?' He shakes his head.

'We usually go to Spain. We're only here now because Mum had an operation and wasn't able to fly.'

'Oh.' This makes me sad. The thought of never seeing him again breaks my heart into a thousand tiny pieces.

'Maybe you can come and stay at our house?' I know my parents would never allow this in a million years, but I smile and nod.

We sit staring up at the sky for what feels like hours as it turns from orange, to red to black.

'Look how bright the moon is.' I've always loved the moon. There's something so magical about it. 'I'll miss you.' It's the only thing I can think of to say that will convey all these feelings I have without telling him I like him.

'Tell you what.' He turns to face me. We are inches apart, our legs almost touching. 'Every August 17th at…' He looks at his Swatch. '…nine thirty. Wherever we are, whoever we're with, we just look up at the moon and think of each other.'

The thousand tiny broken pieces of my heart break into another thousand tiny pieces and I can't stop a little tear from rolling down my cheek.

'Sorry.' I wipe it away. 'Bit of dust in my eye.' I don't want him to think I've gotten all soppy and weird. We have been nothing other than mates this entire week, even if every time I've seen him I've felt sick.

'You know what I said about girls getting weird?' He takes my hands in his. 'I think I'd quite like it if you were to get a little weird.' Could it be? The pieces of my heart bound together again and beat so fast I'm sure he can hear it. 'I mean…' He seems lost for words, something I've never known him to be in all this time. 'Can I kiss you?'

My heart feels like it's going to burst out of my chest at any moment.

'Yes.' I croak and lick my lips self-consciously.

Joey edges closer. Our legs are touching now as well as our hands. He's closed his eyes. Do I close mine? But if I close them, how will I know when he's kissing me? Oh dear Lord. I shut them nearly all the way, leaving just a little gap so I can see what's happening. It seems to take ages. Should I lean towards him as well? Kissing always looks so easy in the movies. Patrick Swayze just started kissing Jennifer Grey in Dirty Dancing.

Then, suddenly, I can feel his lips. They are very soft on mine, warm and with the slightest of pressure. For some reason, I want to open mine and somehow, even though we don't say a word, we both open our mouths at the same time. It feels right and special. After a few seconds I feel something flick the inside of my mouth and realise with slight horror that it's his tongue. What do I do now?

'Sorry, I just thought.' Joey pulls away. He must have felt my hesitation and is now looking at the floor.

'It's ok.' I reassure him. 'I just haven't kissed anyone like that before. Or at all.' His head lifts up again. 'I like it.' He leans in for another kiss and this time I let my tongue wander into his mouth first. It feels nice.

'I can't believe you have to go home tomorrow.' He puts an arm around me, and I rest my head on his shoulder.

'I know, it sucks, doesn't it?'

Chapter 4

My phone pinging brings me back to the present. It's just my daughter telling me they've landed in Majorca. I wish her a happy holiday, slightly pissed off that I'm not there, but these things happen.

I flick through the diary and find a photo of me and Joey taken just before we left for home. The two of us are sitting on the sun lounger, arms round each other, smiling happily with sun kissed cheeks and freckled skin. I look like I've been crying and, of course I have. When I flick it over, he's written *Meet me in our spot*, something he used to say rather than saying goodbye. He sent the photo to me a few weeks later with a card and we kept in touch for a bit. Weekly letters turned into monthly, then to now and again, then to nothing at all. But I still look back with fondness and think of him on August 17th when my memory allows.

I know he became a surgeon and eventually got married. Yes, I stalked his Facebook profile about ten years ago, but I never plucked up the courage to send a friend request. After all, if he wanted to be friends, he'd have sent me one. Then a few years ago, his profile was set to private as I think most people did and now I can't see anything on there.

I carry the box downstairs and plonk it on the sofa before remembering the cup of tea I was making. It's cold now, bits of scum from the tea bag floating on the top, so I tip it away and start again.

Hearing a key in the lock, I turn to find Rob walking in. He looks sad, sadder than I've ever seen him, and I wonder if I have that same look on my face. I remember seeing it a few years ago when our dad died. Even though he'd suffered from dementia for a few years, his death was a surprise because although his mind had failed him, his body, we thought, was a strong as an ox. Turned out he'd been suffering heart disease for years and died of a clot.

You never know what's going on inside your body sometimes. A fact we've discovered once again.

'Do you want a cuppa?' I ask as breezily as I can in the circumstances. He nods as he bends his head slightly so his six-foot six frame can fit under the door. A man of few words, my brother. Why speak when a nod or shake of the head will suffice? 'How are the kids doing?' Rob has three children, similar ages to mine.

'They're ok.' He shrugs. 'They wanted to come, but you know, since Covid and that.' Ah, the dreaded C word. The pandemic that hit us in 2019 and changed the world forever. Lockdowns, school closures, cancelled events. We sort of just live with it now, trying to get on with our lives as best we can. Wear a mask, don't wear a mask, test, don't test. It all became a little confusing in the end, so I just apply common sense and hope for the best.

The problem is that the NHS is still struggling. GPs aren't seeing patients like they used to, so it's a trip to A&E which puts more and more pressure on it. But I have to say, in this case, it's still bloody amazing and everyone that works in our local hospital can't do enough for you.

'It's hard for them.' I say simply, pouring hot water from the kettle into the awaiting cups. 'I've told mine to go on holiday still, no point in everyone missing out and there's nothing anyone can do, anyway.'

'What are we going to do?' I look up as he speaks. His whole body has drooped, his face has fallen, and his eyes are brimming with tears.

'Whatever we need to.' I place a hand on his arm and squeeze it tightly. 'Whatever happens, whatever needs to be done, we'll do it.' I squeeze his arm again. 'For Mum.'

Rob has never coped well with illness and sickness of any kind. Lyn's ex-husband was the same. I'm not sure if it's a man thing or just an individual thing, but they sort of try to ignore it, hoping it will go away perhaps. If they don't talk about it or even think about it, then perhaps they can pretend it's not actually real. This applies to themselves as well as to others. Maybe it's a coping mechanism, I don't know, it just seems daft to me. It is what it is and the sooner you accept it, the quicker you can sort it out. And that pretty much applies to any problem.

'I just didn't think we'd be doing it again so soon.' I completely understand where he's coming from. Losing Dad so quickly just over three years ago was the biggest shock, one I don't think I will ever get over. To know that he no longer walks on this planet makes me so incredibly upset.

With him having dementia, it felt like we had already lost him in a way. He was physically still here, but he was just a shell of the man he used to be. He looked like my dad, sounded like my dad, but wasn't my dad in any way. Like the light was on but no one was home. His brown eyes had lost their sparkle, and he was just existing rather than living.

It progressed so quickly that it took us all by surprise.

Mum started noticing little things in 2013. His usual keen sense of direction became lost to him, and although he was still an expert driver, Mum would have to tell him where to go. He woke up on holiday once, a place they had been to time and time again over many years and did not know where he was.

Then one morning in Spring 2014, after Mum and Dad had been decorating the front room the previous day, he woke Mum up with a cup of tea and said, 'I know that I love you, but I have no idea where I am'. She took him to the doctors straight away and eventually in August of that year he was diagnosed with mixed dementia.

Things were ok to start with. They carried on as normal but by his 70th birthday the following August Mum was finding it increasingly difficult to care for him. He would empty drawers and cupboards, insist that none of his clothes were his, constantly ask where his parents were and when he could go home. He no longer recognised his home of forty years as home.

Mum kept most of it from us and it wasn't until we visited the Harry Potter Studios in December 2015 that Rob and I realised the full extent of Dad's illness.

All of us are huge Harry Potter fans, but I would probably count myself as the biggest in the family. I quite often watch one of the movies as a 'go to' place. It takes me away from the world for a while.

We sat in the First-Class lounge at Coventry train station, Dad was in high spirits, helping himself to the complimentary tea and biscuits. I've even got a photo of everyone sitting in the lounge and Dad is smiling in the background, raising his cup to the camera. We played cards on the journey, chatted, and looked out the window.

The studio was decorated for Christmas and my daughter and niece wore Harry Potter cloaks, swishing around the sets like they were on the film. But Dad looked at everything as if it was a blank canvas. There was not the slightest bit of recollection, even when we turned the corner to see the Hogwarts Express. His face held no excitement or enjoyment, and he would just wander off, sometimes without us knowing.

We still had a good time, but on the way home, Rob and I kept exchanging glances, like we knew something was brewing. Little did we know that this would be the last time we would all be together as a family.

I think it was Christmas Eve when Mum phoned me in a panic. I'd never heard her so upset and frightened. Dad had been trying to leave to 'go home' and as she'd attempted to stop him, he'd pushed her out of the way. We had to get the crisis team involved and eventually after three months and just before my 40th birthday, Dad was removed from our care and placed into an assessment unit and eventually into full-time care. He never came home again.

Rob's phone rang as we walked into the living room.

'I'd better take this.' He said and headed out into the garden where there was always a good signal.

I pulled up one of the smaller tables from the nest of tables in the corner and placed my cup on the coaster that says, *Love you to the moon and back*, plop down on the sofa and tuck my legs off to one side. In my family, all the women sit this way, or as with my mum, she sits with one leg completely underneath. Then when she stood up, she'd complain of her foot and knee aching. 'I'm not surprised,' my dad would say, 'considering the way you sit.'

My tea is far too hot to drink at the moment, I need to wait a good ten to fifteen minutes before it's just right. Unlike my dad, who drank tea or coffee as soon as it was made. I always wondered how he never burnt his mouth. After all, it was practically boiling hot water and had only been cooled down by a little bit of milk and three spoons of sugar. 'But don't stir it.' He would say, 'I don't like it sweet.'

I reach for my keepsake box and take potluck on the next thing I pull out. It's another diary, this time from 1993. The year I turned seventeen and the year I got drunk for the first time. Some of the best years of my life were 1992 to 1994. I stayed on at school to do my A Levels after a whole summer of unsuccessful interviews for jobs. I had absolutely no idea what I wanted to do apart from writing and as our career advice consisted of one appointment and a computer survey where most of us ended up being told we were best suited to being refuse collectors or secretaries, I'd sort of ended up applying for dental technician roles.

So, I stayed on at school and chose history, maths and business studies, eventually dropping business studies because it was the most mind-numbingly boring subject I'd ever experienced with the most unenthusiastic teacher I'd ever encountered. At least I enjoyed maths and history.

But most importantly, 1993 was the year I met Christian Sawyer.

Chapter 5

It was September 6th, my first day back after the summer holiday. As usual, I walked to school. It was only a fifteen-minute stroll. Sometimes if I was running late, I'd take the shortcut over the train tracks then through the entry on Green Road that led onto the school playing fields but having been warned about doing this time and time again by parents and teachers, it was always a very rare occurrence, even though India's house actually backed onto the railway.

I felt somehow older today than the last time I walked to school, perhaps it was because I knew this was my final year of sixth form and big decisions needed to be made about my future and I still didn't have a clue what I wanted to do.

India and Lyn didn't stay on at school. They had enrolled in the college near the city centre and were both studying in the care sector. Claire had stayed on though, taken four A Levels and hoped to be accepted at Warwick University. Me, on the other hand, I just felt like I was passing the time until I actually had to decide.

I classed myself as reasonably intelligent, possibly a little above average, but not as smart as Claire. I lacked the diligence and patience to study for long hours. Dad always said I had a Jack-in-the-box brain. This is because I bounced around from one idea to the next. Nothing apart from an interesting book held my attention for long.

It was a warm day for early September, but I was, as usual, dressed in black. I'd grown my short hair out in fifth year, and it now reached halfway down my back. Mum had stopped trying to get me to wear colours, but the lip pursing still happened regularly. Today I had on black jeans, a black shirt and a burgundy waistcoat. With my dark hair down, I looked like your classic nineties goth. I was anything but though.

Wearing black makes me feel sort of invisible. People always think I'm confident, but I'm not in the slightest. I'm a very funny shape, muscly calves from years of horse riding as a preteen, large flabby thighs and arse, tiny waist and a virtually non-existent bust. Broad shoulders from swimming and permanently rosy cheeks. My hair never ever does what I want it to. It is thick and dark and so usually it's left down, but then gets knotty or I tie it up in a ponytail with a black scrunchie.

The sixth form block is packed when I walk in. The new Year Twelves are busy signing up for this and that, grabbing keys to lockers and generally being sociable. The Year Thirteens on the other hand, my year, are far more subdued. We are the eldest, and if this was America, we'd be seniors now. Like Rizzo from Grease said, we rule the school. Except I don't, nor do I want to. I'm not, nor have I ever been, nor have I ever wanted to be one of the cool kids.

It took me a while to find my group of friends. I flitted about for the first two years of senior school, so when I finally settled down with Claire, Lyn and India, I was kind of friends with everyone. I didn't get teased or bullied, but I didn't get invited to the cool parties either. Like I said before, invisible.

Claire moved away from school in April, so her mum drops her in on her way to work. It's so early though that usually the school gates aren't even open but as we use the back gates, being Sixth Formers, and this is by the caretaker's house, he usually sees her and lets her in. Everyone knows how sensible and trustworthy Claire is, so she's left to her own devices with the entire sixth form building at her disposal, but she just grabs us our favourite table and soft chairs and works on her personal statement for her university application.

At four foot eleven and half, you can't ever forget the half, Claire is petite with a diminutive frame to match. I'm five feet eight in my bare feet and feel like a giant next to her. Even my hands are twice the size of hers. Everything about Claire is tiny, except her attitude. Her attitude is fierce.

'How was your summer?' I ask, plonking my rather light bag on the table and sinking into the empty seat next to her. She's been at her dad's house in America for the whole six weeks, so we haven't even spoken on the phone. It's far too expensive.

'Really good.' She barely looks up from her notepad. She isn't being rude, she's just able to multi-task to perfection. 'He's got a pool now, so I pretty much just spent my days swimming and working on this bloody thing.' She slaps her pen down on the table and looks at me. 'I'm fed up with the whole bloody process if I'm honest with you. I'm never going to get into Warwick, and Mum can't afford to pay for me to move away. So that's me screwed.'

Claire tends to be overdramatic.

'You spent all summer on your personal statement?' I'm in awe of her diligence. I haven't even started mine, probably because I have no desire to go and it's only because our head of year is making me apply that I'm even doing it.

'You need to apply, Charlotte.' He said, having caught me in the common room last year when I'd been doing my best to avoid him.

'But Sir, I don't want to go to university.' This excuse was dismissed with a wave of his hand.

'You're a clever girl. You just need to concentrate more.' He looked at me in that way only teachers can, you know, when they're trying to encourage you. They know they're failing to do so but keep trying anyway. I could see the absolute desperation in his eyes and finally, when I agreed, he smiled and patted my hand. 'There's a good girl.' Teachers can be so patronising sometimes.

'How was Weymouth?' Claire asks.

'Just the same as it was last year, the year before and the year before that.' Creatures of habit my parents are. 'I only went this year because it was the only way I was getting a holiday.' I sighed. 'Next year we need to go on a girls' only trip somewhere.'

'Wouldn't that be amazing?' Claire looks wistfully into the distance.

'Even if we don't get abroad, I've got my test soon, perhaps we could go on a road trip or something.' I've been having driving lessons since I turned seventeen back in April, two a week with my brother's old instructor.

'I thought you had your test in August?' Claire eyes me suspiciously. I'd forgotten I'd told her.

'Yeah, failed it, didn't I.' I was so nervous, I actually failed it three times in one. I got so many minor faults and three major ones. I mounted the pavement during my reverse park and kept on driving, my three-point turn was more like a thirty-point turn and when the examiner had to put his hand on the steering wheel, well, I knew it was all over then.

'Never mind.' She smiles. 'All the best people pass their test the second time round.'

A commotion by the door made the whole sixth form look over.

'I thought she'd failed Year Twelve?' I whisper to Claire as Emma Manning waltzed in. She was dressed as if she was off to a nightclub rather than school, and as usual, a trail of boys and girls followed in her wake.

'Haven't you heard?' I shake my head. 'She's repeating the year. Daddy's one of the governors, so he pulled a few strings and here she is again.'

'Well, at least she won't be in any of our classes.' The bell rings announcing the start of the day and with scraping of chairs and loud chatter, the common room empties as we all head off to registration.

Claire is doing all different subjects to me and is also in a different tutor group, so we say goodbye and speak the unspoken rule of meeting up at break in our usual spot.

There's one big problem with my school and that's just the sheer size of it. Six groups per year for five years and then another two hundred sixth formers and we all have to go somewhere. The buildings sprawl over massive grounds. Science labs, maths rooms, English block, history block, language block, gym, sports hall, drama, home economics complete with kitchens, temporary huts which have been there since before my brother started, tennis courts, football fields, athletic track and of course the dreaded cross-country field. I was so glad P.E. wasn't part of the sixth form curriculum.

Hockey seemed to turn even the nicest girl into something from St Trinian's. Netball was a fight for Goal Shooter or Goal Attack, I was always Goal Keeper due to my height, until one day when we had a new teacher, she gave me Goal Shooter for some reason much to the disgust of Emma and her cronies only to realise that I was actually really good and ended up being asked to join the school team, an honour I naturally declined. I spent five days a week with these people. I wasn't about to spend my evenings and weekends with them too.

And then, of course, the compulsory communal shower. Forgetting your towel wasn't a good enough reason not to have one and being on your period was only valid once a month. Mrs Parkes even kept a record of who was on their period, so we had to think of other excuses. The best thing we found was not actually avoiding the shower, but just running back from the fields as fast as we could, chucking off our top and skirt as quickly as possible, hitching down your bra straps and wrapping your towel round you then just getting your shoulders wet and be drying yourself off before the teacher had even made it back into the changing rooms.

Back to the problem of the size of my school. My tutor room is in the maths block near the entrance to the school and first period today is history and you guessed it, right at the other end of the school. We have five minutes to get to class after registration. Lateness is not allowed, so along with many others, we almost sprint to the other end of the school and make it just as the bell rings.

There's an added bonus to sixth form classes. They are far more relaxed, even some of the classrooms are set up like common rooms and the history rooms are no exception. I grab a seat near the back of the room, close to the window. I love looking out of the window. I hear the clack-clack-clacking of Mrs Bacon's high heels announcing her presence before her actual appearance.

It's then that I see him.

Chapter 6

He's standing outside the classroom, his back to the window, looking at something in his hand. His hair is dark and rests just above the collar of his denim jacket. He looks tall, maybe six feet two or three. He turns slightly so I can see the side of his face now. I've never seen such a handsome profile. His nose is perfectly straight, his chin perfectly sized, and I can infer from his expression that he looks a little lost.

Mrs Bacon taps on the window, and he almost jumps out of his skin.

'Can I help you?' She asks, sliding the window open slightly, a look of sheer annoyance on her face.

'Is this HG1?' He asks and his voice is like hot chocolate on a cold winter's evening, smooth and velvety.

'It is.' Mrs Bacon assures. 'You'd best get in and find a seat.' She slams the window shut. She doesn't like delays of any kind. Even being lost is no excuse for tardiness in her eyes.

I watch him walk towards the entrance to the block and then through the door to the classroom. He is gorgeous, and he knows it. He walks with such confidence and assurance that it actually makes me a little jealous of him. To be so comfortable in your own skin that even in new surroundings, you have no fear of doing something stupid or making a fool of yourself.

I on the other hand, have no such abilities. I avoid any situation where I could possibly be made to look stupid. Anytime we had to give presentations in class, I would be miraculously poorly and then have an amazing recovery the next day. The trick to this was never telling your mum what was going on in school lessons. If she didn't know, she couldn't put two and two together and make the correct answer of four. I rarely skipped school and as there was never any pattern to it, she never thought I was faking it.

Unlike Rob.

Rob developed a mysterious illness one Tuesday morning about halfway through his fifth year, complaints of feeling sick, headache, you know the kind of thing. Nothing life-threatening that the doctor had to be called, but enough pain to warrant a day in bed. Then the same thing happened again two weeks later, nothing during half term and then again.

Dad had to have 'the talk' with him.

Turned out, his usual maths teacher was pregnant, and was attending medical appointments every other week and the supply teacher made them all stand up at the front of class and work out algebra equations on the blackboard, hence Rob's sudden illness.

The mysterious boy is now standing at the front of the class. He has a plain black bag slung over his shoulder and I can just make out various pin badges stuck to it, but they are too far for me to see what they are. They're probably expressions, things like, 'Life's a bitch and then you die.' Not very cheerful, I grant you, but pretty accurate. Now I can see that he is wearing blue jeans, slightly baggy but not oversized, the correct way round, unlike some idiots that have taken to wearing them back to front. Under his denim jacket, I think he's got a Nirvana t-shirt on. I can't see his shoes from here, but I assume they'll be high tops of some description.

'Should I take a seat?' He asks Mrs Bacon, who looks a little taken aback.

'It's normally how it works Mr...?' She waits for an answer.

'Sawyer.' He says, quickly scanning the room. 'Christian Sawyer.'

'If you'd like to take a seat, Mr Sawyer, then I can get on with teaching the class or shall I just wait a few more minutes?' This is, of course, a rhetorical question.

'Shouldn't take me long to get settled.' He says cheekily. 'I can see an empty chair just there.' The whole class laughs quietly, me included, until I realise the chair he's talking about is next to mine.

'Just sit down please, Mr Sawyer.' Having known Mrs Bacon now for over six years and having been taught by her for four, I know this is her annoyed tone. Christian Sawyer, however, is new.

'Won't be a second.' He saunters through the chairs and tables, slings his bag onto the floor and almost throws himself into the chair. 'Christian.' He turns to look at me, his hand outstretched. 'Pleased to meet you.' I've melted into a heap of pheromones by now. Clearly the Lynx effect is working its magic on me.

His eyes are a delicious chocolate brown colour, his eyebrows are perfectly arched and currently one of them is raised slightly and I realise that I haven't answered him.

'Charlotte.' I shake his hand. It's warm but not hot, dry and soft and my head fills with thoughts of how his hand would feel if it was to touch my…

'Can I call you Charlie?' He asks, my thoughts thankfully interrupted. 'I like Charlie.' And suddenly my name sounds like vanilla ice cream on his lips, cool and mellow and Dear God, now I'm thinking about his lips.

'Mr Sawyer!' He turns his attention back to Mrs Bacon. 'Would you like me to arrange some alone time for you and Miss Dean? A candlelight dinner, perhaps? A movie?'

My face has turned a lovely shade of ripe tomato, and I'm trying to shrink into my chair and disappear. The whole class is looking at us and smirking. This is not my normal level of invisibility.

'That's very kind of you but I'm…' Christian really needs to stop talking now.

'How about the both of you meet me here at three thirty and I'll arrange a lovely hour just for the two of you?' Mrs Bacon has spoken. 'Now then, turn to chapter fifteen in your textbooks and we can begin learning about The Russian Revolution.'

'What does she mean?' Christian whispers to me as I flick to the required chapter in the huge A Level History textbook.

'She's given us detention.' I shake my head in despair. 'I've never had detention in my whole life.' I hiss at him.

'Ah shit, sorry Charlie.' He appears genuinely sorry. 'Forgive me?' He looks at me with puppy dog eyes and sticks out his bottom lip. I swear I can see tears brimming.

'It's alright.' It isn't, but what can I do? And after all, it just means I'll do my homework in school rather than at home.

Around fifteen minutes later and I'm listening to Mrs Bacon explain about how Rasputin rose to power and gained the influence he had over the Tsarina of Russia when I feel a warm breath on my cheek. I look over my shoulder and there he is, practically on top of me. The tiny little hairs on my neck are standing to attention and every nerve is tingling. I've known him for less than half an hour and this is the effect he's having on me already.

'I forgot my glasses.' He says, as if this explains why he is so close to me. 'And my book. Hope you don't mind me reading yours.' I sigh with slight exasperation and push the book towards him a little more. This will ensure it is evenly placed between the two of us on the desk. I wear glasses too when I have to. Thick NHS frames that come in a choice of shit, shitty or shittier. They certainly didn't give any thought to teenagers when they designed them.

At my last appointment, the optician said my eyes were getting to the point where I should wear them all the time. The thought horrified me, but I'm getting headaches now from straining my eyes to read the blackboard so I'm seriously considering contact lenses.

'Do you actually have to do that?' I whisper through gritted teeth at him. He's chewing gum and blowing bubbles, and it's the most annoying sound I've heard. I'm not sure whether it's because it's right next to my ear or because it makes me think of his lips again and what else he could be doing with his mouth other than chewing gum.

What's wrong with you? I ask myself. I'm not some innocent girl who's never been kissed. I've had boyfriends, granted none have lasted very long, and we never did more than kiss, but what the hell was going on? Why were all my hormones suddenly firing off in all directions, causing my brain to frazzle? This rendered me unable to concentrate on the riveting facts about Russia in the First World War.

'Sorry.' I can feel his smile rather than see it. Then I reprimand myself for being such a harridan. He's new to the school, might even be new to the area, forgotten his books and glasses and all I've done is scold him.

He's exceptionally quiet for the rest of the class and when we're packing up, I feel the need to explain myself.

'I'm sorry if I sounded like a twat earlier.' This seems appropriate. 'It's just Mrs Bacon can be a bit of a tyrant. I mean, she's a brilliant teacher, but you don't mess with her.'

'It's ok.' He packs his notepad and pen in his bag, and I can now see the badges are mostly band names and photos.

'Do you know what room you're in next?' I'm assuming he doesn't.

'I think I've got a free next and then double maths after lunch.' He's smiling again and my insides are flipping over and over. Please let him be in my maths group too.

'Same here.' I say as nonchalantly as I can. He waits for me to put my stuff away and then falls in behind me.

'You can be my guide, then.' My heart sings a little at these words.

'Are you just doing the two subjects here?' Being a rather large and modern sixth form, we often got students from other schools around the city that came for the odd subject rather than full time.

'I'm hoping to get into English too, but apparently it's full at the moment.' He rolls his eyes. 'We moved here in the summer, and they told us I had a place for all three, but now it turns out I might have to carry on at my old school for English.'

'Bummer.' I'm praying someone drops out of English this very day. Sixth form was going to be a whole lot more interesting this year. 'Wouldn't that be a long way to travel, though?' He looks at me oddly.

'I've only moved from Walsgrave, you know.' He laughs. Walsgrave is another part of Coventry, where the main hospital is. It's slightly less posh than Finham, according to my mum, but then, according to my mum, everywhere is less posh than Finham.

On the way back to the sixth form block, I discover he lives on the next road to me, is an only child with divorced parents, hence the move here, lives with his mum and is eighteen in two weeks. By the time we've sat down in the common room, I'm utterly smitten, picking out baby names and practising writing my new signature, Charlotte Sawyer, in my head.

Chapter 7

'Everything ok?' I ask Rob as he comes back into the living room. He looks pissed off.

'Just work as usual.' He shakes his head, sits down in one of the recliner chairs, and sips his tea. 'Bloody place goes to pot if I'm not there.'

'They should make you manager instead of that useless piece of shit that calls himself supervisor.' Rob works for a small company. The boss is hardly there and leaves everything to the supervisor, who Rob explains on numerous occasions is worse than useless with no customer skills whatsoever. Rob ends up having to chair meetings, meet clients, train staff and visit sites. Yet he gets none of the recognition or the pay.

'Don't have a degree, do I?' He sighs into his cup.

'What the fuck has having a degree got to do with it?' I do get annoyed about this subject. Both my children will be saddled with around forty thousand pounds' worth of debt because the jobs they want to break into require degrees. What happened to good old apprenticeships? Learning on the job and getting paid while you do it. My brother is far more qualified than the other chap. Now, don't get me wrong, I'm not being degreeist, if that's even a word. I just don't see why having a degree ranks above the knowledge and experience that comes from working in the same job for over twenty years.

'I don't look the part and I don't know all the highfalutin words Matt uses.' He puts his empty cup on the table.

'Anyone can put on a suit and spout a few long syllable words, my dear.' I know what Rob means, though. He's over fifty now, happy and long term married. He's got more hair on his chin than on his head and he's on the larger side. We both are. But he is the kindest man you could ever hope to meet. He's not the sharpest tool in the box, but only because if it doesn't interest him, then he's not bothered to learn.

Take his schooling, for example. He went to the same school as me, four years before, but this was a time of teacher strikes and the new GCSE's coming in. He didn't particularly enjoy school and came out with low passes. But when he went to agricultural college, he excelled and received distinctions in every single subject. We were all so proud of him.

I think I fluked my GCSEs if I'm honest. The only exam I revised for was French and I ended up with 2 Cs, 6 Bs and an A in maths. Mrs Belcher, my maths teacher, was so shocked by this that when she saw me walking through the school on the first day of sixth form she came running out of her class, calling my name and congratulating me.

My A Levels, on the other hand, were a totally different story.

Rob's phone pinged again, and he looked up at the ceiling in despair. I recommended he switch it off.

'But…'

'Do they know what's happening today?' He nods at my question. 'Right then, turn it off or at least silence it.' He does exactly this but leaves it on the arm of the chair. 'Put it away.' He looks at me. 'Put it away.' I softly say this time, and he pops the phone into his pocket. 'Today is about us and Mum, more importantly Mum, I grant you, but us too and work will still be there tomorrow and the next day and the next.'

What a thought. I mean, I'm grateful to have a job under current circumstances. Rising food prices, spiralling fuel costs and don't get me started on electricity and gas. First it was Brexit's fault, then Covid, and now it's because of Ukraine. I'm not about to get into politics because I think the whole bloody lot of them are a waste of space. Not one of them is in touch with the real world and real people. They should try and live on a 22k income and see how far they get. But I digress and the point I was trying to make was about working day in and day out, in an endless loop, over and over.

Lately I've had a burning desire to write. I never become an author like I wanted to when I was a youngster. But there's a story whirling in my head and it won't stop. The characters talk to me as if they're real, but I don't know where to start. Actually, sitting down with pen and paper or a laptop might be a good idea, I suppose.

'What time is it?' Rob asks even though he'd just looked at it on his phone a few moments ago before he put it away.

'Quarter to.' I answer with a quick glance at my watch.

'What time are we leaving?' I can see he is impatient to get moving, we both are. The quicker we get there, the quicker we can get this over and done with and move forward, but appointment times are there for a reason and we won't make the time go any faster by looking at it.

'Half past.' The look of helplessness on his face that we have another forty-five minutes to wait reminds me of every Christmas morning when we were kids.

For some reason, we used to put our Christmas sacks at the end of our beds and Santa would fill them with presents while we were asleep. Regular as clockwork, Rob and I would awaken at four and drag the sacks into our parents' room, only to be told to go back to bed until six. Rob would then come into my room and ask what time it was every five minutes or so and I would reply, and he would roll his eyes and drag his feet back to bed.

In the end, probably because we were so noisy and they weren't asleep anyway, Mum and Dad would call us in, and we'd jump onto the end of their bed and start unwrapping. I never did get that Mr Frosty, though.

'Can't we just leave now?' He asks.

'But then we'll just be sitting and waiting there rather than here, and I know where I'd rather be.' Sitting on a nice comfy sofa in peace and quiet is preferable to the cold, clinical, noisy setting of the hospital. 'Put the TV on if you want to.'

He flicks on the TV and starts channel hopping, pausing briefly to see what's on before settling on the news. It's filled with the fight for who the new PM will be, followed by rising prices, the impending drought and rail strikes.

'Is there never any happy news these days?' He asks before switching it off.

'They usually end on something uplifting, don't they?' I remind him. 'It's like here's all the bad stuff we need to tell you, but then we'll try to lighten the mood with a story about a cat playing the piano or something equally as daft.'

'And I'm sick to death of these stories and debates with Rishi Sunak and Liz Truss.' I am in complete agreement with this. 'It's not even up to the general public who's taking over from Boris so what does it matter? They'll pick whoever they want to pick, and we just have to get on with it.'

'Boris hasn't even officially resigned yet, has he?' Rob shakes his head.

'Until he's been to see The Queen, he remains the PM.' He pauses for a second. 'What time is it now?'

'Ten to.'

'Honestly, I need to do something.' He stands up, knocking his thankfully empty cup onto the floor. 'I'll mow the lawn.' He heads out into the garden once again and I can hear bashing about as he tries to find the lawnmower, then swearing when he can't find the cable, then the eventual humming noise as he walks up and down the grass.

The grass doesn't even need cutting. It did a few weeks ago. However, the record high temperatures last week and the lack of any real rain have made the lawns dry and brown. The brief shower we've just experienced won't have helped, but at least he's doing something…er…useful.

I'm not like my brother. In fact, I'm not like any member of my family or even my friends, but I have this ability to not worry about things. And I don't mean that I'm blasé about things and don't care, but I just don't worry about something that doesn't need to be worried about.

Worrying is a such a waste of energy and emotions. Of course I prepare for things and think about things but sometimes, the unthinkable never happens and you end up exhausted with night after night of lost sleep. I'm not explaining this very well.

So…for example…my dad was the biggest worrier I have ever known. He would literally worry about having nothing to worry about. But what if the car breaks down? What if the washing machine stops working? Both things that can happen at any time or might never happen. You can't carry every spare part of a car around just in case it breaks. Save money if you can, get AA cover, prepare as much as possible for life's ups and downs, but worrying night after night? It's of no use at all.

And today is a prime example.

I have no control over what is happening today in any way. No one has. Not one person on this planet has any control over what is happening. So I ask you now, what on earth is the point of worrying about it? What if this happens? What if that happens? Well, if this happens, we'll deal with it and if that happens, we'll deal with that too and if nothing happens, then we'll carry on as we have been.

We could be in line for the shittiest news ever, the worst possible news we could imagine at this point in time. Or, by some miracle, it could be bloody amazing, and we can all heave a huge sigh of relief but me having been worried about this day for the past two weeks will make absolutely no difference to the outcome.

Nobody else seems to see this though, or maybe they just can't help but worry.

I check the time again and there's still half an hour till we have to leave and an hour before we need to be there, so I wash the mugs, leaving them to dry on the draining board. I wave at Rob from the window. He looks a little more relaxed I notice.

Sitting back down on the sofa, I pick up the diary from 1993 again and continue where I left off.

Then I remember my first detention and I start to blush.

Chapter 8

Christian has already amassed an entire group of admirers by the time second period has ended and I've all but been forgotten. Emma made a beeline for him during break and had to be dragged away from him for her lesson. The 'top lads' have also made their claim on him, and he is now ensconced as one of the cool kids. It's obvious he is at home with them and fits in straight away. I'm a little sad, but it's not like I'd chosen our wedding song and picked out the menu now, was it?

I don't normally see Claire throughout the day except for break. She has completely different subjects to me and often spends lunch working in the library. Sometimes I sit with her when I want company, usually during the summer because for some reason the library is always cool. Normally I grab lunch from the snack bar or if I've been up early enough, I'll have made a sandwich. Today I am fully prepared and even before the bell has rung to signal lunch I'm heading outside to my usual spot.

This is my favourite place to be invisible and how no one else has found it is beyond me. Mind you, I only discovered it by chance in my fourth year after there'd been a storm, so maybe it wasn't visible before then.

It's just on the first of the school playing fields, quite close to the gap you squeeze through from the entry on Green Road.

I've pulled branches about a bit to cover the entrance some more and they've grown again over the years, so it's now my little haven. I didn't even tell Claire, India, and Lyn when I found it. I just wanted it to be mine.

Being invisible has its uses. I just pass by people unnoticed most of the time and today is no exception. I used to always check before stepping into the huge Laurel hedge, but now I don't bother, I'm like a ghost most of the time. The girl they all know the name of but rarely speak to unless during lessons. Some might say I'm lonely, in a way I am, but I also like my own company and the company of books.

Please don't feel sorry for me though, this is only a school thing. This is because apart from Claire, everyone else I was good friends with didn't stay on at school. We've had such an influx of new people that they've already got their groups and at sixteen years old, you very rarely start new ones.

I push the branches aside and there it is. Clearly an old P.E. storage shed, long forgotten. How it's still standing is beyond me. Perhaps the hedge has protected it from the worst of the weather all these years. When I first found it, the door was hanging off the hinges, so I borrowed one of Dad's screwdrivers and fixed it the next time I came.

Over time, I've snuck things in, so now there's a few cushions and a blanket for the floor. I keep them in a black bin bag when I leave, just in case. I cleaned the window as best as I could and most days there is enough light to read by.

Settling down on my blanket with my book and ham sandwich, I block out the sounds from the field and find myself transported to the late 18th century and the Wideacre estate in Philippa Gregory's novel, Wideacre. She is a new author to me. I found the book on the library shelf last week and have been totally enthralled by it. I only started it last night and I'm already halfway through. It feels as if the author is writing from personal experience. The way she tells the story of Beatrice and her struggles with being a woman makes me feel as if she actually knew her and lived in those times herself. So vivid are the descriptions that I can almost see and smell the sights.

'So this is where you're hiding?' I jump out of my skin at the voice and spill the sip of coke I'd just taken. This is another reason I wear black; it hides stains.

Christian is standing in the open doorway, his arms above his head, leaning on the top. A little bit of light peeks through and casts sunbeams on him making him look like an angel. Perhaps that should be the devil, because the thoughts I'm having right now are far from angelic. He is smiling at me and although I'm annoyed at being interrupted, maybe even at being found, his smile is making my insides do weird things. Any anger I feel is quickly turning to something else, something I'm very scared of feeling.

Is scared the right word? I'm not scared of the feelings per se, just scared that this, whatever this may be, feels like it has the potential to consume me. I've only known him half a day, and he's already found my secret spot and if he smiles at me again, the way he's doing right now as if he can see into my very soul then I'm afraid I will not be responsible for my actions.

'I'm not hiding.' His raised eyebrows prove me wrong.

'Of course you're not.' He hasn't once stopped looking at me. 'Can I come in?' I'm happy that he's asked, although as its school property, technically he can do whatever he pleases.

How to answer?

Yes, of course, far too forward. No, far too abrupt.

'If you want.' A very nonchalant answer.

He steps in and the already small space is filled with his presence.

'Can I sit down?' He is having to bend his head slightly, and I scooch along the blanket a little to make room for him. He makes a big deal of actually sitting down and in the end, he's sitting facing me. The space isn't the largest when it's just me, so the added person of above average height means suddenly it's a little cramped. Or is that because it's him? 'What are you reading?'

I show him the cover of the book and am pleased to see him nod.

'Do you read?' I ask. Not many boys his age do.

'I'm into comics myself.' He pulls out a notepad from his bag, leans up against the wall, resting the pad on his knees, and starts sketching.

'Are you an artist?' I'm intrigued. 'Can I see?'

He holds the pad up in front of me. 'I'm not very good.'

My mouth drops open at the sheer exquisite drawing before me. It's like a scene from the recent Batman movies with Michael Keaton, dark and brooding. But the hero isn't a man in a suit, it's a woman in a cape.

'That's amazing.' Amazing doesn't seem good enough.

He turns the pad back to him and takes out his eraser. 'I can't get her face right.'

'Maybe move onto something else for now.' I suggest. This always helps me. No good bashing your head over and over again, just come back to it.

'I can see exactly how I want it to be, but it just won't come out right.' This is exactly how I feel about art, although my talent runs to stickmen and symmetrical thatched cottages. I can see the picture clearly in my head, like in third year art. I wanted to draw a beautiful crystal ball on a purple background with clouds swirling inside. I ended up drawing a football and needless to say, I didn't take art at GCSE. 'Maybe you're right.'

I can sense his frustration, but he puts the pad away and looks over at my lunchbox.

'Have you eaten?' My appetite disappeared the moment he arrived, so there's still half a sandwich and a packet of Monster Munch. He shakes his head. 'Help yourself.'

He grabs the Monster Munch and places one on his finger before biting off each claw individually.

'Want one?' He asks, offering the packet towards me, but I shake my head. 'How long have you been hiding in here then?'

I give him a look. 'I told you. I'm not hiding.' I start reading again, but it's no use. I've read the same sentence five times now, and it is not sinking in.

'Ok then.' He bites another crisp. 'How long have you been coming here and sitting on your own to avoid the company of others?'

He's hit the nail on the head and I can tell by the way he's trying not to laugh that he knows it.

'I found it in fourth year but started using it more from last year.' I answer the question without admitting that he is totally correct.

'Any particular reason?' He's already finished the packet of crisps and is reaching for my drink. I don't like sharing cans and glasses with other people, even family, but I feel powerless to stop him, especially as his hand brushes against my thigh and now I seem to have lost the capability to speak coherently. Thankfully, he continues to talk, which gives me time to compose myself. 'I mean, you seem a perfectly normal, well-balanced individual. Kind from what I can make out so far. Friendly. You've already shared your book with me and now we're sharing lunch.'

'I don't like people.' Not true, I do like people. I love my family and friends, but I just can't be doing with the falseness that is teenagers. Everything seems to be about who can go out with the best-looking guy or girl. Who can be the most popular? Who wears the most expensive clothes? I just can't be doing with any of it. I'm never going to be popular or good looking, and the thought of spending fifty quid on a pair of trainers just because they're Nike or Adidas is beyond me.

He nods. 'I don't like people either.'

'Yeah right.' I look at him. He is dressed in the perfect 90s clothes. His hair is slightly too long on top to be fully on trend, but he is so good looking that you forgive him. 'You're perfect.' I realise I have said this out loud when he smiles lopsidedly at me, and a tiny dimple appears in his left cheek.

'This.' He waves a hand down his body. 'All for show. It's what's in here that counts.' He places a hand on his heart. 'And how you use this?' He taps his head with the tip of his finger.

I'm about to ask him more but the warning bell for end of lunch sounds and I hurriedly pack away.

'Do you want to follow me to maths?' I ask as we quickly stuff the blanket and cushions back in the bag.

'I'd follow you anywhere.' He whispers and as I look up and meet his gaze, I'm hypnotised. He leans towards me, his head bent slightly to one side. The bell rings again and I jump out of my skin.

Chapter 9

'How much homework?' Christian moans as we step out of maths and begin the long walk back to the history block for detention. The entire school, apart from a few like us, is heading in the opposite direction, out to the school gates, and it's like trying to push your way to the front of a concert. I pull him to one side in the small area under the maths block and wait for a space.

'Patel does like to pile it on, I'm afraid.' I've done half of the exercises already though when Mr Patel was called out of the class and everyone else messed about and talked. Even though Christian was sitting at the next desk to me, he was soon immersed in football talk with the lads, so I kept my head down and worked through the exercises we'd been set. Claire, India, Lyn and I were off to the cinema tonight, so the less work I had to do the better.

Mum and Dad weren't keen on me going out on school nights, but at seventeen years old, there wasn't a lot they could do to stop me, and it wasn't like I was out getting drunk every night like some. No, it was usually an evening spent at India's or Lyn's house or if something good was on at the cinema. Or a trip down to the local video rental shop.

I spy a gap in the throng of pupils and push Christian ahead of me.

'You're telling me he does.' He says, stepping in by the side of me as soon as humanly possible. 'What with the essay Mrs Bacon set, plus I've got reading to do for English tomorrow, looks like I'll be up all night.'

'The jump to A Levels is so bad, isn't it?' I'm now super happy that I only take two and not three subjects.

Mrs Bacon is waiting for us when we arrive but seems eager to leave.

'I haven't had time to set anything for you, so just get on with the essay from class and I'll be back in a moment.' She didn't even wait for us to sit down before she walked out of the door in somewhat of a hurry.

'Wonder where she's off to?' Christian asks, flopping down in a chair and pulling out his drawing pad.

'She's head of history and has a tutor group, so probably a meeting or something.' I purposefully sit down a few desks away from him and start on the essay.

'You're not actually working, are you?' He looks over at me, his pencil tapping lightly on the desk.

'May as well.' I shrug my shoulders. 'I'd only be doing it at home, so what's the difference?' He looks at me oddly, as if I've answered some eternal question about how the universe came to be or something like that.

'Why have I never seen it that way?' He puts his pad away, picks up his bag, and moves a chair right next to mine. 'Can I share your book again?'

'Do I have a choice?' He shakes his head.

'Not really.' He's leaning on the desk now, his head on his right hand and his face turned towards me. 'Did you know you do this funny little thing with your mouth when you're concentrating?'

Obviously, I am completely unaware of this little foible. 'What do I do?' I'm in a slight panic that I might drool or be sitting with my gob wide open.

'You kind of bite your lip.' His gaze is fully on my mouth, and I can feel the heat rising into my cheeks. 'It's quite sexy, really.' No one has ever said that anything I do is sexy and I'm a little unsure as to how I'm supposed to react to this.

'Thank you.' I whisper, not trusting my voice in any way, keeping my attention firmly on the book in front of me whilst concentrating so hard not to bite my lip.

'Have you ever been kissed before?' I clearly reek of inexperience if he feels the need to ask me this, and my pride prickles a little.

'Of course.' I'm still not looking at him, my gaze, fully on the chapter about the assassination of the Russian Royal Family, but I couldn't tell you one fact about it because I'm not actually reading any of the words. I'm trying so hard to keep my breathing steady and my heart beating at a normal pace lest he should hear the blood pumping around my body to the beat of Let's talk about sex by Salt n Pepa.

'I mean a real kiss.' He has somehow edged closer to me, that's what happens when you don't keep watch. 'A kiss that makes your toes curl, a kiss that makes you want to…' He trails off.

'Do what?' I stupidly ask and even more stupidly raise my head to look at him. His eyes seemed to have turned a dark chocolate colour. His mouth is slightly open, and he quickly licks his lips before raising an eyebrow and winking slowly and deliberately. 'I can honestly say I've never had a kiss that's made me want to wink before.' I deliberately choose to ignore his innuendo. We are, after all, in a downstairs classroom, with the windows open to the school and Mrs Bacon due back at any time.

'Touché.' He says, leaning back into his chair.

'Any further questions?' As soon as the words fall from my mouth I realise he meant to kiss me. Now my head is whirring with thoughts of his lips on mine and I could kick myself for wanting to get one over on him. Trying to be a smart-ass doesn't always pay off.

'Have you ever had sex?' He's clearly seen another opportunity and is back leaning on the desk.

'No.' I state clearly and confidently. 'Not that I haven't had the option.' I don't want him to think I'm a prude or anything. 'Have you?' I ask, closing the textbook and turning my full attention to him.

'That would be telling.' I never understand that answer. It's such a cop out.

'Kind of the point.' If we're going down this road, then he can answer just as easily as I can. 'I ask a question, you say yes or no, simple.'

'It's complicated.' He says, and I can see he's squirming slightly.

'But it's not.' I feel suddenly empowered because his cool demeanour has slipped a little. 'You either have or you haven't? I haven't, not even really got close if we're being brutally honest.' Why did I say that? 'You've either had sex with a girl or you haven't.' I quickly turn the subject back to him. He seems reluctant to answer. 'Oh God!' Realisation dawns on me. 'You're gay, aren't you?' Just my luck, falling for a gay guy.

'Not last time I checked no.' He pauses as if he's deciding whether to say something else. 'I did think I might be once a few years ago.'

'Really?' I've never met anyone my age who was gay or even who thought they were gay.

He nodded. 'Turns out I fancied his Action Man collection rather than him.' He laughs and I'm not sure if he's telling me the truth or not. I don't know him anywhere near well enough to tell.

'So?' I go back to the original question. 'Why is it complicated?'

'Her dad caught us.' He looks down at his feet.

I can see how mortified he is by this, but I can't help giggling. 'I'm sorry, that must have been awful.' The giggle turns to laughter and luckily, he smiles.

'We were parked up outside her house, just before Christmas it was. I'd only just passed my test and was driving my mum's car. It was the first time we'd been out together in it. We'd been seeing each other for a while and things got a little steamy so we moved onto the back seat, next thing I know, the door is wrenched open, and he pulls me out of the car, trousers round my ankles and roars at me never to see his daughter again.'

'What did you do?' I've stopped laughing now.

'The only thing I could do?' He smiles. 'Drove off as fast as I could and didn't go back.'

'That wasn't very fair to the girl now, was it?' I didn't like the end of this story.

'I tried to phone her the next night, even waited outside her college, but she just ignored me.' He shrugged. 'She was dating some university student the next week.'

'Well, at least you tried.' I'm comforted by his words, then laugh again as I remember. 'Your trousers were really by your ankles?'

'Oh yes.' He nods and joins in the laughing this time.

'Well, I'm glad to see you've been using your time wisely and putting you into detention was not a complete and utter waste of my time.' We haven't heard Mrs Bacon return. 'I assume you've both finished your essays and clearly need another one setting.'

'We're really sorry, Mrs Bacon.' I put on my most apologetic face.

'I've a good mind to make you stay longer, but as it is, I've got an emergency at home so you can leave early, and that essay had better be worthy of an A.' She stormed out.

'Thank God for that.' Christian stands up and hands me my textbook. 'Let's get out of here before she changes her mind.'

It always fascinates me how quiet schools are when nearly everyone has gone home. It's like you shouldn't be there and every little sound seems to echo through the empty buildings. The main gate is still open, and we trudge up the steps and onto Wall Lane. All too soon, we are outside my house.

'Are you in tomorrow?' I ask him, not wanting today to end, but he shakes his head.

'Not unless they suddenly find me a place in English.'

'But we have maths in the afternoon.' Like I'm worried he'll miss a lesson and it's not purely for selfish reasons that I want him to come to school.

'Maybe you can help me catch up?' He's looking at me that way again. 'See you later, Charlie.' And then he's gone, across the road and through the entry into his street.

Chapter 10

We're late. How we manged to be late after sitting around waiting for almost an hour is beyond me. First Rob couldn't find the keys to lock up the shed, but after turning the house upside down we eventually found them in the garden waste bin where they'd fallen out of his pocket and get sucked up into the lawnmower and then tipped into the bin. Luckily, with the grass being so dead, there wasn't much to look through.

Then we got caught by one of the neighbours, who despite us telling them time and time again that we were running late and really needed to leave, insisted on talking for England.

'Mum will kill us.' I keep checking my watch as Rob drives us. He's better at speeding than I am. 'I just hope they wait for us to get there before talking to her.'

Thankfully, there is hardly any traffic due to it being the school summer holidays and also the middle of the morning. Luckily we spot someone just leaving and grab their space much to the disgust of the BMW driver who I could see had spied the same space but was currently stuck behind a car that was driving in and out of its space trying and failing to straighten up.

We sprint to the entrance, hooking face masks onto our ears as we go. The revolving doors are way too slow, and we accidentally cause them to stop by being too fast and touching the glass.

'Oh for fuck's sake!' Rob mutters.

'More haste, less speed.' It's one of Mum's favourite sayings, along with 'a stitch in time saves nine' and 'that really takes the biscuit'. I never understood the last one. Although, I'd happily take the biscuit, it means 'that really takes the piss', unless everyone has taken the last biscuit and now there is none left. I can't believe I've just worked it out.

'Are we going to the ward or clinic?' Rob asks, standing in front of the massive board with numerous departments and arrows pointing in all directions.

'We won't be allowed on the ward as it's not visiting hours and it's already ten minutes past the appointment time, so we'd best go straight to the clinic.' We don't run, even though we're dying to. It's something that just isn't done, running in hospitals. You see them doing it in Casualty all the time, but in real life I've never seen one person actually run. Rush, yes, but not run.

The clinics are as usual packed. We sanitise our hands before going in and head to clinic four, where mum is sitting in one of the chairs looking mightily pissed off. She's dressed in her usual attire of top and trousers, and like most, has a face mask on, but I know underneath that, her face will be thin and drawn. Unlike my brother and I who have quite round faces, even without being overweight, Mum has always had a long, thin face. The minute she loses weight, it disappears from her face rather than her hips and thighs where the actual fat is.

She's aged these past few weeks and I still can't quite believe it's only been a few weeks since this nightmare began.

'Where have you been?' She scolds, sounding like Mrs Weasley in The Chamber of Secrets film, and we sit down next to her like naughty toddlers and not the grown-up adults with children of our own that we actually are. That's the magic of a mum, though, isn't it? The ability to make you feel instantly like a child again when you do something wrong, but also to raise you up so incredibly high when you do something right.

'Sorry Mum.' We both mumble into our chests.

'We lost the shed keys.' Rob tries to calm the situation, but these are not the right words. Mum looks at him as if we've lost the keys to Fort Knox and not just the shed that has nothing other than a patio set, lawn mower, and a few garden tools in it. And anyway, what's with the we? 'But we found them again.' He says hastily. 'That's why we were late.'

Mum has this thing about making sure everything is locked up. I think it stems from Dad. He was a little obsessive about certain things, and I think they became increasingly problematic as his dementia took hold. My daughter stayed with her while attending university. She stayed just a few nights in the week so she could catch the bus in the morning rather than struggling for parking spaces. If Mum had to go out, she would always say 'make sure you lock up and don't lose the key'. The girl was eighteen years old and had been locking up our house for a good four years and had never lost a key in her life.

If she's out for the day or on holiday, we are forbidden to go in the house in case we forget to lock the door after us. Why would we forget to do that? We've been homeowners for over two decades. Does she think we walk out of her house and say, I know, let's leave it unlocked? And the car! Jesus! How many times we walk back to the car to check it's locked is beyond me.

Mum and Dad had a keyless one a few years ago. Whenever they went anywhere, Mum would have to walk away with the fob and Dad would wait by the car and then check it was locked when she'd walked far enough away.

'They never run on time, anyway.' I realise straight away from the seething look Mum gives me that these words are even more hurtful than the ones Rob said. But it's always been that way. Even though I'm not the eldest, I think, because I'm the girl and usually more sensible than my brother, I should be impeccable at all times. Unfortunately, I am only human and also inherited my dad's couple lack of thinking before opening my mouth.

'That is beside the point, Charlotte.' The way she says Charlotte makes me wither a little inside. However, I bite my tongue and try to see it from her point of view.

She's worried, possibly the most worried she's ever been in her entire life. Of course, we've had Dad's dementia to deal with, her father's brain tumour years ago, but this is personal to her. This is her health, her life, and nothing makes you feel your mortality more than something like this.

I take her hand and squeeze it reassuringly. 'Sorry Mum. We'll do better next time.' For I know that no matter what we hear today, there will be a next time. Maybe many, many next times over a short period, maybe just the occasional one over a long period. But we all know that the hospital will soon be a regular place to visit.

It's already been like a second home this past week as it is. I took Mum to A&E due to the immense pain she was in, and they admitted her so they could do further tests and keep her pain under control. I only work a few minutes away, but visiting time is six till eight and I finish at four, so I wait around before going to visit. With the cost of petrol as it is, I can't afford to drive home and drive to the same place again two hours later.

Rob and I alternate days, so Mum always has a visitor. There's nothing worse than being in hospital and everyone else has someone come in and you're just sitting there alone like Billy no mates. Another saying I don't understand. Who decided Billy would have no mates? Why couldn't it have been Eric?

We sit and watch person after person get called. Mum is patiently fidgeting; Rob looks at his phone every two minutes and I'm trying desperately to think myself away to anywhere else but here.

'That's two people now that came in after us and have gone through.' Mum hisses at me.

'Because there's five consultants in this one clinic, Mum.' I don't know how many times she needs this explained. Every time she goes to the doctor or the hospital, it's the same old thing.

'Anne Dean?' Then suddenly her name is called and the three of us stand up in unison and walk towards the front. 'I'm Jade, one of the urology and oncology nurses. I'll be with you at your appointment today and then we'll have a little chat afterwards if you've got any further questions.

Am I the only one that heard the word oncology? Granted, Mum is slowly becoming quite deaf although she won't admit it and Rob is giving his best, I'm not worried in the slightest impression but surely they heard it? Surely, they know what oncology means.

Jade leads us into the room where a nice man of my age is sitting. He's wearing a face mask so we can only see his eyes, but there is something familiar about those eyes. Mum sits down in front of him, Rob to her side and I'm sitting opposite with the man's back to me but Mum and Rob's faces towards me. I'm not sure if it's a good thing or not because I can see the screen clearly.

He introduces himself to Mum and Rob, but I didn't hear his name as he is so softly spoken, then turns to me.

'And are you a daughter, a daughter-in-law, perhaps?' He asks. Jesus, where have I seen those eyes before?

'This is my daughter, Charlotte.' Mum says.

'Charlie.' I correct her and he looks momentarily taken aback before composing himself and giving his full attention to Mum.

'So, Mrs Dean, do you know why you're here today?' He asks, flicking through scans on the screen. My knowledge isn't great, but I think he's looking at lungs, because of the way they're inflating and deflating.

'To tell me my scan results and possible treatment.' She speaks quietly, and I can hear the nervousness in her voice.

He flicks through some more screens before turning it slightly so Mum and Rob can see. This time I know exactly what I'm looking at. Mum's kidneys. You can't mistake the shape of kidneys except in this instance there's only one white, healthy kidney shape on the left-hand side of the screen. On the right is what appears to be a grapefruit-sized shadow. There's a tiny little bit of white at the bottom and the top, and I know exactly what he is going to say next.

'Unfortunately, Mrs Dean,' No nice sentence ever begins with the word unfortunately. The word unfortunately has never been accompanied by a piece of good news 'It is as we suspected.' I can see Mum's face fall behind her mask, her eyes look down to the ground then flick straight back to the consultant as if determined to meet the actual diagnosis head on and I know that she will fight. 'You have a twelve-centimetre mass on your left kidney consistent with kidney cancer.'

My whole world collapses around me and I wish I was back reading my diaries.

Chapter 11

I didn't have to go into school till third period today, so I slept in, read a little and worked on my essay for Mrs Bacon. If you have more than one period free in Upper Sixth, you can attend or stay home depending on which way it falls.

Maths seems empty without Christian, and I'm struck by how much I keep thinking about him. I only met him yesterday, but my thoughts seem to drift towards him at random moments. Like last night, for example, at the dinner table. There we all were having a perfectly normal Spaghetti Bolognese., normal for our house being that Mum has to cook two different sauces because Rob refuses to eat sauces of any kind and heaven forbid if there's a vegetable on his plate. Little does he know; Mum has painstakingly chopped onion and carrot so fine to mix in with his Oxo cube that he hasn't the foggiest idea.

There we all are, munching away, Rob talking about work, Dad talking about work, Mum talking about work and all I can think about is Christian and how my name sounds when he says it and how he gets that little dimple when he smiles and the cute way, he raises one eyebrow.

The home bell rings, and I head out of the gate with the crowd and take my usual route. A beeping horn startles me and I look round to see someone waving from the driver's seat of a black Ford Capri. I'm not wearing my glasses, so I have to squint a little to bring their face into focus. It's Christian.

'Shit!' I'm wearing the same clothes I had on yesterday. What on earth will he think?

'Fancy a lift?' He steps out of the car and beckons me over, so I cross the road. Today he is wearing black jeans and a plain white t shirt, and my word he looks gorgeous. 'I finished after third period so thought I'd swing by and pick you up.' He says, assured that I will say yes. I will say yes, obviously.

'But it's only a fifteen-minute walk.' I didn't say I'd say yes straight away.

'We could go to The Milk Bar by the ford?' He suggests. 'Mum and I went there in the holidays.'

'Is it still open? I thought they closed at the end of August?' The curse of British weather. Things that only open for the summer season because obviously once September and October arrive, we become recluses and don't venture out.

'I'm sure the sign said open till the end of September.' He walks around the side of the car with me and opens the door. 'We could take a drive there and see.'

'Why not?' I step into the seat as elegantly as I can and put my bag by my feet. He's got Radio 1 on, Steve Wright in the afternoon and the opening bars to Boom Shake the Room belt out of the speakers as he gets in.

'I love this song.' He turns it up a little more, turns the key and with a roar, the car comes to life. It isn't far to The Milk

Bar, only about five minutes in the car, down a little track that's almost hidden from the main road. Christian parks the car, runs round to my door and opens it just at the same time that I do.

'Thank you.' I'm not used to chivalry, and it makes me smile. 'Shall I leave my bag in the car?' I don't really want to be carrying it.

'You can pop it in the boot if you want.' He flicks open the car boot and I deposit my bag in the back after removing my purse. Thanking my earlier self for remembering to actually take her purse to school and also remembering to put actual money in it.

'I haven't been here in years.' It's not somewhere I ever think to go. The girls and I usually head into town or grab sweets and pop from the corner shop when we're renting a video, but actually going out for a drink is a bit of a rarity. 'I think my grandad brought me a few times, and I used to have a Mini Milk and splash in the ford.'

'Mum said she came here all the time when she was younger, so we took a walk one day and found it.' We walk side by side, close but not touching.

The walk only takes a few minutes and before we know it, we've come to the little ford, which is basically a few concrete steps in a stream. No one knows exactly why it's there, there aren't any buildings or anything so there's no need for a crossing of any kind but maybe there was at one point, after all, you don't just build a little café for the sake of it.

'It hasn't changed a bit.' The Milk Bar is exactly as I remember it, effectively a little shack in the middle of nowhere with a blue and white striped awning and a few tables and chairs dotted about.

We head up to the counter. 'My treat.' Christian announces. 'What will you have?'

I'm not hungry at all, something that is becoming a regular occurrence in his presence, so I opt for a portion of chips and a cola float. He orders the same, pays and then leads us over to a table right by the stream. There's no one else here apart from an older couple enjoying a cuppa with their Labrador fast asleep under the table.

'How was English?' I ask as we wait.

'Boring.' He says. 'I didn't have anyone to talk to.'

'I find that very hard to believe.' I scoff. 'You're Mr Popular wherever you go.'

He leans forward and takes my hand in his. 'I meant no one that I actually wanted to talk to.' We sit there for a few minutes, he's absent mindedly stroking the back of my hand with his thumb and it's doing crazy things to my insides. I wish I could tell him to stop, but ultimately, I don't want him to.

'Two portions of chips and two cola floats.' The lady announces with a smile and plonks everything down carefully onto the table and he lets go of my hand.

The chips are thick cut and crispy, just how I like them, and I smother my portion in salt and vinegar whilst Christian just sprinkles salt and then opens a few sachets of tomato ketchup. The cola floats have come in tall ice cream sundae glasses, but there's slightly too much cola in them and so the ice cream has frothed over the top. They taste delicious all the same.

'Good news though.' He takes a huge sip of his cola to bring the level down and I do the same. 'I've got a place from next week; someone has dropped out.' I can't help smiling. 'You're grinning like The Cheshire Cat.' He says, and I know that I am.

How can he be having such an effect on me after such a short time? Like my whole happiness suddenly depends on him being around.

'I feel like The Cheshire Cat.' I catch his eye as I take a bite out of a chip, and he winks at me. 'Ow! It's hot.' I resist the urge to spit it out and instead put up with the burning sensation, wafting my hand in front of my face as if that will do anything to cool the inside of my mouth and swallow it down as quickly as I can causing me to choke.

'You ok?' He asks, full of concern.

'I'm fine.' I say even though my throat is on fire and my eyes are watering. 'I must look an absolute mess.' I should imagine I have mascara running down my cheeks. It's about the only makeup I feel confident enough to put on, that and green concealer to tone down my red cheeks.

He leans over the table towards me. 'You look beautiful.' He whispers, cupping my face in his hand and wiping my cheek with the top of his thumb.

'I don't. I look a fright.' I look down at the table.

'Stop doing that.' His voice is soft. 'Stop returning compliments and putting yourself down all the time.' He moves his hand under my chin and lifts my face to look at him. 'You are the most beautiful girl I've ever seen.' I go to scoff, then remember his words and end up snorting like a pig instead. He laughs gently. 'You are irresistibly flawed, like all of us are. You're funny and kind and I haven't stopped thinking about you since the moment I saw you walking through school yesterday.'

'You saw me?' I ask. 'When?'

'Just after the bell had rung for first period.' He smiled. 'You looked like you wanted to be anywhere but where you were and I watched you walk off with your head down, trying not to be seen. So I followed you.'

'What do you mean you followed me?' I'm confused now. 'You were heading to history?'

'I have a little confession.' He lets his hand drop from my chin and suddenly looks very sheepish. 'I don't take history.'

'What do you mean, you don't take history?' I look at him suspiciously, turning my face to the side and looking at him from the corner of my eye. 'You asked if it was your classroom.'

'Actually, I asked if it was HG1, which it was.' He lifts his shoulders up to his ears. 'I just wanted to meet you there and then, so when Mrs Bacon told me to come in, I did.'

'You don't take history?' I ask again, even though I know the answer and he shakes his head. 'Is that why you didn't have your textbook or seemed remotely interested in actually doing the essay?'

He nods. 'Although I'm a little scared of what Mrs Bacon will do to me when I don't hand in the essay.'

'You do take maths though?' I ask, recalling that he had a maths textbook.

'Yes, and English and chemistry.'

'And you sat through a whole history lesson…' I'm trying to make sense of it in my head. '…and a detention.' He nods. 'Just so you could meet me?' He nods again. 'You could have met me in the break, you know, or lunch? After school even.'

'Seems a bit daft when you say it like that.' He sits back in his chair and runs his hand through his hair, causing his fringe to flop straight back over his eyes. 'It was kind of a spur of the moment thing.'

'Do you often do spur of the moment things?' My drink has come to an end, but I slurp the last bit up noisily and try to look slightly flirtatious with the straw.

It must have worked because he leans on the table again. 'It has been known.'

He is inches away from me and I can hear the blood pumping round my body and my heart thumping in my chest.

'Shall we go for a walk?' I suggest, suddenly very conscious of the fact I am absolutely desperate to kiss him, but not with people watching. Of course no one is paying any attention to us, but I'm acutely aware of them.

'Sounds good to me.' We push our chairs back and stand up in perfect sync with one another. I lead the way, heading up along the path and away from The Milk Bar. The path is quite wide, lined with tall, thick trees that have created a leafy canopy over the top, so it feels almost like a tunnel. Despite the wide path, we walk as close together as possible, our arms by our sides, and I can feel his hand brushing gently against mine with each step.

After a few minutes, I feel him hesitantly take my hand and as I don't resist, he links his fingers through mine. We walk a few more steps before he suddenly stops, turns towards me and takes my other hand in his. And now I know, without a shadow of a doubt, that he is going to kiss me.

Chapter 12

We stand in total silence for what feels like an age, yet I know it is only a few seconds. We are holding hands at the tips, facing each other, looking into each other's eyes. He is a few inches taller than me, so his head is slightly tilted. My mind is racing with random thoughts, like will his lips be cold after the cola float? Will he taste salty after eating the chips? Does my breath smell? And of course, the age-old question, what if it's crap?

And I don't mean what if I'm rubbish at kissing or he is because after all you can practise these things, it's fun. But what if, when our lips touch, there is absolutely no connection whatsoever? That it's like kissing a fish, not that I've ever kissed a fish, but you know what I mean. Wet and cold and absolutely no chemistry at all.

Is he thinking the same? I have no idea, but he's looking at me as if he's trying to work something out.

There's no rush and no hurry. We're completely alone with nothing to do and nowhere to go other than just be in this moment. However, the urge to get it over and done with is wrestling with the desire to savour every second because, after all, you only ever get one first kiss with anyone and wherever possible it should be a memorable one. I want to look back when I'm older and remember these moments. I might be with Christian in the future, but the likelihood is I won't be, but I still want to look back with fondness and be able to recall this warm, fuzzy feeling that I'm feeling now.

The only way to describe the look on his face is quizzical. A mixture of amusement and confusion, and I totally understand it. It's like the most confused you've ever been but you're actually quite happy about it. You know ultimately that they want to kiss you. All the signs are there but there is this nagging, niggling little doubt that maybe, just maybe you've read it completely wrong and when it actually happens, they'll laugh at you, tell the whole school and you'll be known as Little Miss Never Been Kissed, or some other such nonsense.

All my worries were totally unfounded.

I don't know who made the final move, me, him or a mixture of both? I think we both sort of lean towards each other at the same time. There is a slight panicked look in his eyes that I feel mirrored in mine, as if at any moment the other might pull away.

But neither of us does.

His lips on mine were the sweetest, most delicious thing that could ever happen up until this moment. I was right; he tasted slightly of salt as I'm sure I did, but it was the closest I had ever come to heaven in my entire life, and I wouldn't have changed a thing about it.

There was no pressure to deepen the kiss. We didn't even move our heads or our hands. We just stood there kissing, as the trees watched, our fingers entwined, enjoying the closeness and the silence.

The kiss came to a natural conclusion, and we broke apart, silently looking into each other's eyes as we pulled away. We still stood there, holding hands, just looking at each other, and I've never felt such a connection to another person in all my seventeen years.

'Right then.' He said, as if he'd been waiting for his voice to return.

'Right.' I reply. There is no point in any other words. 'Shall we?' And I'm not actually sure what I'm asking. Shall we head home? Shall we carry on walking? Shall we kiss again?

'Yep.' He simply says, but as we don't know what he's agreeing to, we still don't move.

The sudden change in weather takes the decision away from us. As a few drops fall we head back to his car, holding hands and chatting about tiny, insignificant things when all I want to do is talk about when we're next going to see each other and how I'm going to cope being away from him.

By the time we reach the car, the few droplets have turned into a downpour and when we come out of the canopy of trees, we are instantly drenched and start running and squealing at the same time. He still opens the door for me, and I jump in as he runs round and gets in his side, slamming the door and shaking his head.

His hair is already flat on his head, and he sweeps it back, laughing and starting the engine at the same time. I watch him as he drives. It seems to come naturally to him, or maybe it's just because he's been driving for almost a year. For me, I'm still concentrating on looking in my mirrors, checking blind spots and now and again I still have to look down to see what gear I'm in or if I've put the handbrake on or off fully. The fact that the car is either stationary or moving should give me that answer, but you know, it's me.

I look at my watch and am shocked to see that it is almost five o clock. 'Shit!'

'What's the matter?' We're just turning onto the main road that leads to mine and his.

'Mum is going to freak.' I should have been home at three thirty. I never go anywhere after school unless I've already told her. I even phoned her yesterday from the public phone in the school foyer, so she knew I was in detention and would be late. 'You'd best drop me here.'

'I'll drop you home. It's no trouble.' He keeps driving.

'It's best Mum doesn't see you.' He looks crestfallen at this.

'Are you ashamed of me?' He asks, pulling over and turning to face me.

'Oh God, no.' And I'm not. 'Not in the slightest, but you need to understand something about my mum.' Now how to explain it? 'Obviously I'm late home from school, she's going to be worried because I haven't told her I'd be late so if she sees you dropping me off then it will be entirely your fault for corrupting her innocent daughter and she'll take an instant dislike to you before she's even met you.' He seems to understand, but I need to say more. 'Whereas if I walk in, all apologetic, she'll be a bit shouty to begin with, but then it'll turn to concern that I'm soaking wet.'

'Sounds a bit mad, if you ask me.' He drives on a little further and pulls up in his road, just before the entry that will lead through to my street. There are four roads on this side of the highway and there is an entry through the middle of them so you can walk through without having to walk up and down the whole road. It's quite ingenious of the person who thought of it. I've not seen it anywhere else. Lyn lives in a crazy area; you walk miles just to get to the end of the road and then again to make it to the shop on the opposite side. A little entry halfway along would have made such a difference.

'It is, I know, but that's how she is and how she's always been.' I'm reluctant to get out of the car for a variety of reasons. One, I'm about to get absolutely soaked. I am currently a little bit drenched but soaked is a whole other level. Two, I'm almost certain to get shouted at, not something I relish. And three, the most important one. I've got to say goodbye to Christian. 'I take it your mum isn't as strict as mine.'

He shakes his head rather enthusiastically. 'She was when I was younger, but since I've been driving and also the fact that I'm eighteen soon, I think she knows that I'm not going to do anything stupid or get myself in a situation I can't get out of. Dad is the same. I have a curfew, neither of them let me stay out past midnight on a school night, but weekends and holidays etc…I can pretty much come and go. I just leave a note or when I'm at Dad's I'll write on the chalkboard where I am, and he writes back.' He shrugs. 'It just works.'

I long for that kind of freedom, but I know it will be quite a while until I get it. They're not as strict with Rob, never were, but even less so since he's been working and he's also five years older than me and a boy.

What they say is true, girls are always treated differently than boys. We can't walk down the road at night on our own. In fact, I very rarely walk anywhere on my own, to be honest. Always make sure someone knows where you are, don't go off the beaten track, don't get in cars with strangers. Ooops! Here I am sitting in a car with a virtual stranger. Yet he isn't. I feel like I've known him forever, yet I know nothing about him except his name, birthday and what car he drives.

I don't even know his address.

'Which house is yours?' I rectify that problem immediately.

He points a little way down the street. 'That one there, number ninety-eight.'

It looks like any other house on these streets. They are all a bit different, but they are basically the same. Driveway, semi-detached or terraced houses with the odd detached house on the 'posh street' which backs onto the woodland. Mum always complains that they could have bought a house on that street but Dad wouldn't have the higher mortgage even though they could afford it so they ended up in the house next to Mum's parents and I can honestly say that I love having my grandparents next door. I see the Deans maybe once or twice a month, but not a day goes by when I don't see Nannie and Grandad Hunt.

'Looks nice.' My hand is on the door handle, but I still don't open it.

'You can come in if you want?' Oh, how I wish I could, but I shake my head.

'Mum will be mad enough as it is.' I look at him and he looks as disappointed as I feel. 'Maybe I could pop round later?' I suggest. 'Show you what you missed in maths.'

'I'd like that.' He places his hand on mine and squeezes.

'I'd like that too.' I smile at him and suddenly all the awkwardness is back. 'I'll see you later then.'

'Later.' He agrees and the look he gives me is a promise for the future. Summoning all the courage I can to leave him, I pull the handle, push open the door and run down the entry. As predicted, Mum is livid, but her words fall on deaf ears because all I can think about is later.

Chapter 13

'Now, we've booked you in for five weeks from tomorrow. I've had to move someone to October, but unfortunately your need is currently greater than theirs. I'm happy for you to go home on pain medication, but you need to self-isolate from next week and then three days before you'll have a Covid swab and then you basically lock yourself away with no visitors at all.' I know Mum isn't listening. She's nodding her head as if she is but I can tell that the information won't be sinking in so I'm taking it all in so I can tell her later. Rob has gone into shut down mode. 'Luckily your other kidney is perfectly healthy so when this is removed, you'll be able to live life just as before.' He explains a little more and then gives Mum the authorisation form and she signs it without question. We say goodbye and then have a further meeting with Jade to make sure we fully understand everything. Rob doesn't speak and Mum is a very grey pallor, as if all the colour has drained from her face.

We head back up to the ward Mum is currently on. Jade accompanies us to tell them she can go home, and we pack her things and make small talk as we wait for her medication and discharge.

Rob walks on ahead to fetch the car but I know he is making an excuse to be on his own, like I said before, he doesn't cope well with illness. It isn't that he doesn't care, of course he cares, it's his mum for goodness sake but it's like if he ignores it as much as he can it might go away perhaps or at the very least, he wouldn't have to actually face it.

It's just me and Mum. She walks so slowly now, even slower than me. She still hasn't fully recovered from breaking her ankle last year, but now, cancer is taking its toll and she is permanently exhausted.

'You should have let me bring you down in a wheelchair.' We are making desperately slow progress, and I worry this walk will be too much for her to cope with. She's holding onto my arm as we walk, and I can feel how frail she has become. She's never been a big woman, but now any fat she had seems to have disappeared completely and her skin is literally hanging off her bones.

'While I can walk, I'll walk.' I'm not sure if her determination is a good or a bad thing.

'At least the car will be right outside when we get there.' It's another five minutes before we reach the entrance and there is Rob, as close to the revolving doors as he can get. I feel the relief wash over me and Mum.

It's a quiet drive back. Vic Minett is on BBC CWR. Rob used to go to school with her and she's playing Bryan Adams, Run to You. Mum is in the front and I'm in the back. My mind is whirling with everything we've just been told and also, quite randomly and really of no importance, the doctor. He looked so familiar and clearly recognised me when he heard my name, but I couldn't quite place him.

'Wasn't the doctor lovely?' My mum says. 'He was so kind to us and didn't rush us in any way at all.' It was true, he hadn't, and this is why, Jade told us afterward, he usually ran over in his appointments. He always made sure his patients and their family were completely happy with everything and he'd answered all the questions before sending them home. If that meant the next person was late, then so be it, because the next person might have lots of questions too or just need more time to come to terms with everything they've just been told.

'What was his name again?' I ask, hoping this will help.

'Mr Martin.' It means nothing to me at all. 'He had lovely, kind eyes.' I'm thinking again about those eyes. It was really all I could see with the mask on apart from his hair. I'd have guessed he was around my age, but honestly, who can tell these days? 'I feel very safe knowing he's going to be doing the surgery.'

'Did he say what the recovery time would be?' Rob asks. I knew he hadn't been listening properly. We'd been told no less than three times.

'I'm not sure what he said.' My mum looks at me through the mirror on the car's sun visor and I think to myself, not for the first time and probably not for the last time, that it's a good job I don't switch off. That no matter what the situation, I listen, ask questions and take it all in. I can forgive Mum, of course; it was a shock to her but imagine if I was the same as Rob. None of us would know anything about the next few weeks.

'He said if all goes well and according to plan, you'll be in surgery for around two to three hours.' I think this is amazingly short considering the scale of the operation, but then I suppose he's done it hundreds of times and it's just a simple case of taking something out, there's nothing to go back in if you get my meaning. 'Then he said most people are in for three to five days.' This is my worry. Mum hates hospitals with a passion, and I worry she will be asking to come home after the first day.

This is, of course impossible and impracticable. But Mum is as stubborn as they come and if she wants to come home, she'll damn well make sure that she does, regardless of the fact that she'll have one, possibly two rather large and sore incisions depending on how the surgery turns out and that she'll have just been through a major operation and will need almost constant supervision. I made a note to talk to her about this at some point.

Honestly, I don't think she realises how much this operation will affect her, or maybe it just hasn't quite sunk in yet. She's rather lucky to have reached her mid-seventies with no major illnesses or traumas. I don't even think she's ever had an operation before. Then there's me, C-Section, followed by appendicitis six months later.

'Home sweet home.' Mum says as we pull up on the drive. I notice that Rob has left the engine running as he gets the bag out of the boot, and I help Mum into the house.

'I'll be off then.' He says, giving Mum a peck on the cheek and what I can only describe as an *I'm sorry, I can't do this* look to me. I give him a reassuring smile; I mean, what else can I do? Scream and bawl at him, insisting he stays. That's just not me and although I'll moan about it to my friends later and they'll agree with me and rage with me. Lyn will say how her brother is exactly the same. It won't change anything.

I wave him off from the step and go inside. Mum has already fallen asleep, so I cover her up with a blanket and wonder when our roles reversed and she became the child and I the parent. It would be a totally different kettle of fish if Dad was still here. Mum would have been waited on hand and foot and wrapped in cotton wool but both Rob and I work with families of our own and we just can't be there twenty-four seven as much as we would want to be.

Locking the front door as quietly as I can, I step out of the back, through the gate and into my Nan's house next door. She's ninety-eight now but as independent as they come. I'm dreading telling her. Mum and I have tried to prepare her as best we can. The doctor has previously tried to warn us it could be something sinister, but I've actually got to sit down and tell her that her eldest daughter has cancer.

She doesn't take it well, of course she doesn't, and we just sit for a while in silence as she takes it in. A bit like when we told her Dad had died, it was such a shock for her, for all of us, but she hadn't seen him since he'd been placed into care as she's housebound herself, suddenly, she would never see him again.

I make her a cup of tea and answer any questions that she has and try to reassure her as much as I can.

'Well, you'd best be off then.' And I know that this is her cue that she wants to be alone. She's not being rude, she does it with everyone, rarely with me I have to say, but I've just given her some terrible news and I'm not sure she knows how to process it. My grandad, her husband, died of a brain tumour, and it was the most awful thing our family had been through up until that time. Then, of course, we had my other nan's dementia and then Dad's and now this.

No matter how old your daughter is, regardless of whether she is eight or eighty, a mother's feelings will be exactly the same. Just as that age old saying goes that no parent should ever have to bury a child. She couldn't face Dad's funeral. She'd known him for the best part of sixty years, and he was as close to her as a physical son could be, maybe even closer because there wasn't ever the stress that a mother and child relationship can have. Instead, there was just pure love and respect.

I sneak back quietly into Mum's house. She's still asleep, quietly snoring away, so I pour myself a glass of orange juice and curl up on the sofa next to her, tucking my legs under me as I always do. I'm not risking the TV, I don't want her to wake up until she's ready, so I reach into my box, trying not to make any noise and softly pull out my diary again.

My phone vibrates with a notification from my daughter. Thankfully, it was still on silent from the hospital. I fire off an explanation of what has happened, softened of course, because although she's an adult this is her grandmother, and I don't want her worrying or getting upset when there is absolutely nothing that can be done other than to follow the doctor's advice. It's something we're going to be living with now, probably for the rest of Mum's life. Even if she comes through all this, there is still the possibility that it will come back or that it will have spread.

She sends me a sad face emoji, and I send her a kiss back.

Suddenly, I see a little blue circle next to my Facebook messenger. I have turned the notifications off and barely use it. It's probably some random stranger wanting to be my sugar daddy or some such other nonsense. Honestly, does anyone ever fall for these?

I open the app and it all comes flooding back to me. I smile at the memories, for I now know exactly who Mr Martin is.

Chapter 14

'I don't care what you promised, Charlotte, you're not going, and that's the end of it.' Mum is still angry with me, and I look at Dad over the dinner table.

'She's only going to do homework in the next street.' Dad says. Rob is keeping his head down, but I can see he's trying not to laugh.

'With a BOY!' She says boy so loudly I think the whole neighbourhood can hear her.

'What does it matter whether it's a boy or a girl?' Dad asks, pouring more gravy over the chicken even though he's already had about a pint. The chicken is particularly dry today, probably because of my lateness, but no one dares to say anything in case we get our heads bitten off and the whole thing thrown in the bin. Dinner is dinner, after all.

'Because.' I smile inside because I know she doesn't have a proper answer.

'Just make sure you're home by ten and don't walk through the entry because it will be dark.' Dad says.

Isn't it weird that we don't walk through the entry in the dark? I must have walked through that entry hundreds of times in my lifetime. People go through it at all times of the day but suddenly, after dark, it's a whole new ball game.

'In fact,' Dad continues. 'I'll pick you up at ten.'

'Ah Dad,' I put my fork down noisily. 'He'll think I'm a right baby.'

'Either your dad picks you up and walks you home or you don't go?' I know better than to argue and pick my fork up again, exaggerating the cutting of my chicken to make a point and am rewarded with a look from my mum through half-closed eyes.

'I won't knock on the door,' Dad says. 'I'll just wait by the entry.' I smile at Dad. He always knows how to let us both have our own ways.

'Honestly, Jerry.' My mum shakes her head. 'You give in to her far too easily.' She chews on a piece of chicken, trying not to show us how hard she must chew. 'I don't know why you can't go and do your homework at India's.'

I can't help but laugh. 'For starters, India doesn't take maths and isn't even in sixth form.'

'Claire's then.' She suggests.

'Then someone has to drive me and again she doesn't take maths.' Mum doesn't look impressed by my answers. 'Christian is new to the school, and he's missed maths today, so I said I'd go over what we did in class.'

'Well, he doesn't sound very suitable company if he's already skipping school after two days.' She starts collecting everyone's plates and then scrapes leftover food onto one plate before piling them all up.

'Actually, he was at his old school today for English because they didn't have space here but now they do.' Mum purses her lips and stands up, the plates clunking together as she does.

'Just don't blame me when you come home pregnant.' She storms into the kitchen. Dad rolls his eyes and Rob, who has been holding his laugh the entire time, spurts the sip of pop he's just taken all over the table.

This is one of Mum's favourite things to do. Giving a warning of dire consequences if we're doing something she wishes we weren't. Things like don't come crying to me when you break your leg, or you'll be sorry when you end up dead. That particular one was for Rob when he wanted to buy a motorbike which Mum was totally against.

The warning about coming home pregnant is a stark one and one that has been drilled into me from so many angles: parents, school, TV, magazines. Teenage pregnancy is so frowned upon in my generation. Even though I'm still a virgin, I panic if my period is late and with me, that's most months. I think to myself, well I must be pregnant then, but how? Perhaps a sperm escaped and swam through the swimming pool. Or there was one on the toilet seat in that restaurant that had shared facilities and it leapt up into my cervix. Absurd, I know, but when your period has a cycle of anything from thirty-four days to fifty-six, you do have these random thoughts.

Mum comes back in with a Viennetta, which is sliced into four. The problem with Viennetta is that one minute it's too frozen to get your spoon in but seconds later it's too soft and the lovely swirly ice cream on the outside is melting. But we battle through.

Rob and I tidy away the dishes and start the washing up while Mum and Dad watch the news. I don't like the news. It's all doom and gloom. Hospital waiting lists reached a million last month for the first time and there's something about a new Independence Party that wants to break away from the European Union. How can we do that? Are we upping the country and moving it to Australia or something? Surely the very nature of where we are means we'll always be in Europe. Dad had to explain that it meant they wanted out of this pact thing that lots of countries were in. I just nodded my head. I never understood politics.

I'm eager to head upstairs and get ready. Rob can see this, and he lets me off with the drying up. We get on so much better now he's an adult. We fought like cats and dogs growing up. I used to steal his Action Men for Sindy's boyfriend or hide his Subbuteo men in his old fort that Grandad Dean made for him.

Now we have the dilemma of what to wear. I'd ring one of the girls, it's after six so I'm allowed because it's cheaper but that will waste precious moments and will undoubtedly lead to an hour on the phone telling them everything that's happened today, then the other two will get upset because I didn't tell them at the same time. Honestly, I wish there was a chat or something where you could all see what was going on. I know there's mobile phones now; they seem amazing but they're so expensive, I very much doubt I'll ever be able to afford one and the thought of Mum being able to ring me at any time, no matter where I am? No, thank you very much.

It's a challenge to choose just the right outfit. We're not going on a date so it can't be too much but the same old jeans and top that I usually wear will not cut it. I've also got to be careful about looking like I've tried too hard because I don't want Mum to know how much I like him. Our living room leads straight off the hall and there's a door right by the front door and Mum, of course, sits right by that door and it's always open. It's also right in front of the window so she can see exactly what's going on in the street.

I opt for my dark indigo wash jeans, a white bodysuit and a denim shirt over the top. I wouldn't normally wear the bodysuit because they are the worst kind of hell when you need the loo. Whoever designed them clearly did not intend them to be worn for long periods of time. Undoing the poppers every time you need to go and then the hassle of getting them fastened again when not in the comfort of your own bedroom. However, it makes my boobs look good and I don't intend to be using the toilet at Christian's house because…you know…what if he hears me?

The denim shirt is currently buttoned up almost to the collar and I've refreshed my mascara and attempted to brush my hair. It's really starting to annoy me now if I'm honest, and I'm seriously considering getting it all chopped off. I take a last look in the mirror, satisfied that this is the best I'm going to do with what's on offer. I'm no Cindy Crawford, but I'm happy. I grab my favourite black heeled, Victorian style boots and sit on the bottom stair, lacing them up.

Another look in the hallway mirror and then…

'Don't forget…' Mum begins, and I can see her reflection in the mirror, looking at me over her puzzle book. 'Your dad will be outside at ten o' clock, not a moment later.'

'Yes, Mum.' She nods as if satisfied with my answer and then finally I can leave.

It's not quite seven, so it's still light, but give it another month or so and we'll have the long autumn nights again. I quite like autumn though, all the burnt orange and red colours as the leaves fall and that slight chill in the air, but spring is my favourite season. That promise of new things to come, all the trees and flowers budding with life once again.

Suddenly, I felt sick as I walked. Not sick as though I'm about to hurl at any moment, but that light feeling in your stomach that you get when you're nervous. Like someone filled it with clothes and switched on the spin cycle. I've never felt this way about a boy before. Not even when Greg Leigh asked me to dance at the fifth year's leavers disco and I'd had a crush on him since the third year.

He'd been all hands and kissing him was like sucking on a boiled sweet except I was the sweet. Sometimes, crushes are best left that way. He's in sixth form now and when I see him, I can't believe how I fancied myself in love with him. Teenage hormones have a lot to answer for.

Spitting the piece of mint chewing gum into a tissue, I throw it in the bin at the end of the entry and breathe into my cupped hand, holding it close to my nose to check for any offensive smells. There's nothing, of course. I undo all the buttons on my shirt and then tie the ends together, so it sits just above my waist, a tip India told me about. It helps define the waist more and draws attention to the bust area.

I'm almost there and I can feel my hands getting clammy, so I wipe them on my jeans and then…I'm there. Outside his house.

Pull yourself together, girl. I scold myself in my head. *It's obvious he likes you, or he wouldn't have asked you over and he certainly wouldn't have kissed you earlier.* But to an insecure, unconfident, slightly overweight seventeen-year-old, it is not obvious, not in the slightest. What if it was all a mistake? A misunderstanding? A bet? Or even worse, pity?

I almost turn and head home, but then I see something move in the front room and before I even have a chance to knock on the door, it's open and Christian is standing there, beaming at me. He's dressed as he was before, and I silently curse myself for changing and making me seem overly keen. But from the look in his eyes, I can see that I have totally made the right decision.

'You look…amazing.' He says, running his hand through his hair. I'm starting to realise he does this a lot. Perhaps it's when he's nervous.

'Thank you.' Do I compliment him back? I didn't earlier when he was in the same clothes so it would seem a little odd to do it now.

'Are you going to invite the poor girl in Christian or just leave her standing on the doorstep all night?' A female voice enquires.

'Sorry.' He looks sheepishly at me before standing aside and allowing me to pass. 'Come in.' He takes me into the living room, it's almost the same set up as my house except our living room and dining room are one adjoining room. 'This is my mum.'

His mum smiles at me and holds out her hand. 'Pleasure to meet you, Charlie.' She looks very much like any other mum I know. Mid-forties, soft features, dressed in unassuming colours with permed hair that looks like it's all but grown out. Only Claire's mum is different. Claire's mum is cool.

'Is it ok if we go in the snug?' Christian asks.

'Of course.' His mum nods. 'Don't work too hard.' She says, turning her attention back to the weather forecast.

Christian takes my hand and leads me back out into the hall, down into the kitchen and out what would have been the back door. At our house, we have a shed here, but at Christian's, it's a small passageway with two doors leading off.

'Oh shit!' Its then that I remember. 'I forgot my books.' He must think I'm a total idiot.

'It's ok.' He says, leaning in for a kiss. 'I wasn't intending on studying much, anyway.'

Chapter 15

Just as his lips are about to touch mine, I panic. 'I could go home and get them.' *Why did I just say that?*

'You could.' He suggests, his lips hovering above mine.

'We could just use yours; I think I remember the exercises.' He lifts his head up and looks at me enquiringly.

'Come on then, let's do maths.' He opens the door in front of us, reaches in and switches on the light. The room is gorgeous. There are huge bean bags on the floor, an enormous TV on the wall and in the corner…

'Is that an arcade machine?' I rush straight over to it. 'Space Invaders!' I can't believe it, a full-size space invader machine just like the ones you get in the arcades on holiday.

'My dad does house clearances and stuff and he found it a few years ago in a pub.' He pops a coin into the slot and instantly the lights and music start, and the familiar pew pew sound begins. 'Come on then.'

I grab the other joystick and dash between the buildings, pressing the button as I go.

'Quick, shoot it.' I shout as the spaceship zooms across the top of the screen for bonus points.

'Missed it.' He says as he waggles the joystick.

'You're shooting your own barrier,' I shout.

'It's a trick I learnt.' I watch out of the corner of my eye as he shoots a sort of channel through the middle of the building. 'See.' And I can see, he's able to shoot at the aliens but remains pretty much protected until a rogue shot falls straight down the middle accompanied by a boom sound.

'Not such a clever trick.' I laugh, concentrating on my own side. We're down to the last line now and they are going so fast it's almost impossible to hit one. 'No!' I scream as the alien lands on top of me.

'Still want to do maths?' I shake my head. 'It's not due till Friday, we can do it tomorrow night instead. He laughs and puts another coin in the machine.

After a few games, my hand is hurting. 'Enough.' I say as he goes to start a new game.

'Fancy a drink?' I nod and he heads over to a part of the room I hadn't noticed before. It's sort of a little nook, hidden away slightly by the L shape of the room, and I can see what appears to be a bar. 'Hooch?' I'm a little shocked that he's allowed to just grab an alcoholic drink at home but then remember that he's almost eighteen. I hesitate, imagining what Mum would say. 'You have had Hooch before?' Of course I have, it's basically alcoholic lemonade.

'Yeah.' I walk over to him and see cabinets of different spirits, bottles of mixers and all kinds of glasses. 'Wow, you could open your own bar.' We have a very small drinks cabinet at home. Well, it's not even a cabinet it's just part of the huge sideboard in our dining room with a pull-down door. All that's in it is a bottle of Tia Maria that Mum was given at Christmas and a few Babychams.

He opens two bottles of Hooch and hands one to me. It's sharp and cold and slightly fizzy on my tongue.

'Crisps?' He throws a packet of Walkers ready salted at me which I fail to catch due to the fact that I was taking a drink at the time, and it hits me in the face. 'I'm so sorry.' He's by my side in an instant and takes the bottle off me.

'It's ok.' He looks so incredibly upset. 'It was just a packet of crisps. No harm done.'

'I can be a right twat sometimes.' I really can't understand why he's so upset. 'Are you sure you're ok? I didn't catch your eye or anything?' He cups my chin and gently guides me under the light. 'It looks ok.' He says after examining my eyes more closely. He lets go of my chin.

'You could take another look.' I felt daring all of a sudden. A few sips of Hooch can't have affected me that much. Perhaps it's just his closeness.

'I did hurt you, didn't I?' He is all forlorn again.

'Not in the slightest.' Well, that didn't go according to plan.

'Sorry for being a bit of dick.' He flops down on one of the bean bags and sips his drink. 'It's just that I'm a bit paranoid about things like that.'

I pick my bottle back up and sit down next to him. 'Why?'

'My cousin took a chunk out of my eye when we were five with the corner of a yogurt pot.' I can see now why he's upset. 'We were looking in the fridge at my nan's house, I was standing behind him looking over his shoulder and he pulled a yogurt out and the edge of it flew straight in my eye. It didn't half pour with blood.'

'I bet it did.' I'm slightly horrified by this. 'Did you go to hospital?'

'Yep, in an ambulance and everything.' He says this bit with a smile. 'One of my earliest memories, to be honest.'

'I've never been in an ambulance.' It's one of those things you always think will be exciting as a child but as you grow up you realise that being blue lit in an ambulance is because you're seriously ill, bleeding and sometimes both. 'Can you see ok?' Surely he can, he wouldn't be able to drive if he didn't.

'It left me partially sighted in the one eye, but I can do everything pretty much the same. I just wear a contact lens to correct the vision or my glasses.' He puts his bottle down on the floor. 'You can see the scar if you look close enough.' He leans towards me as if this is an invitation and I put my bottle down next to his and lean in.

'That white chunk on your iris?' I ask. I've never seen a scar on an eyeball before. He really has got lovely eyes. 'It looks like someone forgot to finish colouring in a picture.'

He laughs. 'That's a good way of describing it.' Our faces are level, our eyes looking at each other. 'Is it ok for me to kiss you now?' I know why he's asking; my hesitation earlier must have been really off-putting for him.

I swallow loudly and lick my lips. 'Yes.' Was that my voice just then? It sounded so much deeper than usual. 'I was just nervous earlier; you know and then…' He puts a finger on my mouth then takes it away, quickly replacing it with his lips.

This time there's no salty taste, just him and it is as sweet and delicious as I remember. He places a hand gently through my hair and cups the back of my neck, his thumb resting between my cheek and my ear. His other hand is resting on my thigh, and I can feel the heat from it burning through my jeans as if he's on fire.

My hands have taken on a mind of their own and are currently around his back, pulling him closer to me. He lowers me gently back onto the bean bag, so we are side by side, kissing me continually the whole time. I make the first move with my tongue. I want to taste all of him, every single part of his mouth, and he matches my movements with his own.

I've never felt more alive in my entire life. Every nerve in my body is tingling and I want to be as close to him as I can. I'd climb inside his skin if I could. His free hand has moved from my thigh and is now positioned just above my hip. Somehow, he's managed to find bare skin where my bodysuit has risen and my jeans have fallen down slightly. It feels as if that part of me might catch fire at any moment.

He isn't doing anything with his hand other than it just being there, but the electricity is coursing through my veins, and I feel like I might explode. His kiss deepens even further, and I match it, strength for strength. His lips never leave mine and I can feel his hair has fallen and is brushing against my face slightly. I know this will annoy him slightly, so I reach up with my hand and smooth it back.

'Thanks.' He says and I can see him smiling at me as I sneak a quick look at him before he reclaims my lips. I feel like I could just lie here all night, kissing him. Our bodies have moulded together as if they were carved from the same piece of stone. I fit into him perfectly, like the last piece of a jigsaw puzzle.

'What time is it?' I ask, suddenly noticing how dark it had gotten outside.

'I have no idea.' He answers against my lips. 'Does it matter?'

I wish that it didn't. Dear God, I wish that it didn't. 'My dad's picking me up at ten.' I'm not sure if it's the mention of my dad or the fact that I have to go home that is the passion killer, but I feel him sort of flop against me as if he's been holding himself back and now, knowing that it's coming to an end, he can let go again.

'Really?' He seems incredibly surprised, and I remember that he doesn't yet know my parents.

'It was that or not come at all.' I smile awkwardly at him. 'I think it's a little punishment from Mum for being late earlier.'

He looks at his watch. 'Nine thirty.' He reads off and sits up as if a brilliant idea has suddenly come to him. 'I'll walk you home.'

'You don't have to.' Although I very much want him to.

'Listen…It will be bonus points for us.' I cock my head to one side. 'If you get home early, then that will look good on both of us and means we respect the rules etc… and if I walk you home, it shows what a gentleman I am.'

I smile at his thinking. 'It would throw Mum off the scent a bit.' It's a good plan and the more I think about it, the more I realise it's a great plan.

'Throw her off the scent of what?' He looks at me in all innocence.

'That you're not a gentleman in any way and all you want is to keep me here and kiss me all night.'

'Guilty.' He says. 'And if we're quick, we can get another ten minutes in.' I laugh as he kisses me again.

We hold hands as he walks me home, not really saying anything, just enjoying the night and the quiet that it brings. He kisses me gently as we reach the doorstep, wishes me goodnight, and then is gone. I unlocked the door and walked in just as Dad was putting on his shoes and Christian was right; it definitely earned him some brownie points.

Chapter 16

I wake up and have no idea where I am. The room feels
unfamiliar yet homely all at the same time. Discombobulated
is what my workmate Kim would call it. It's one of her
favourite words. She's a cracking friend is Kim, one of those
people that I just instantly clicked with. We've only actually
met once, just before Covid and she's worked from home
since then, so we only chat over phone calls and team
meetings, but I could honestly chat to her all day, every day.

Then I remember I'm in my brother's old room. It feels so
odd. I've never slept in this room before but there's only a
desk and chair in my old bedroom now, so it was this or the
sofa. Mum told me to go home, that she would be ok, but I
didn't want her to be on her own after receiving that kind of
news. Truth be told, it was me really that didn't want to be
on my own.

It feels like morning. I can see a little light framing the
outside of the curtains, but they must be thickly lined
because not even the smallest ray is getting through. I look at
my mobile, eight thirty. I haven't slept this late in months.
Then I realise that today is a workday, and I haven't told my
boss that I won't be in.

He's very sympathetic of course, I mean, what else can you
say? I've worked for them since I was twenty, so it's not like
I'm messing them about. Unfortunately, my role as HR and

payroll manager is strictly office based, whereas Kim is publicity and sales, which can be done from anywhere.

I peek in on Mum as I head to the toilet. She's sound asleep and I'm not going to wake her, so I make a cup of tea and take the fish and chip wrappings outside to the bin while it mashes in the pot. I decide to sit outside and soak up the early morning sunshine. There's something so tranquil about just sitting and being. Not scrolling through social media and TikTok videos, but just you, nature and a cup of tea.

'Why didn't you wake me?' Mum asks, walking out into the garden and sitting down next to me. 'I never sleep this late.'

'Then perhaps it's time you did.' I say, getting up and making her a cup of tea and myself another one. 'You've got cancer Mum.' And as I say it, it hits her hard.

'I know.' She looks into her mug and blows on it gently. 'I've been silly for not admitting it haven't I?'

'Not in the slightest.' I say. 'Do you not think I was hoping we'd get there yesterday, and the doctor would say, I'm really sorry Mrs Dean but we've got your scan mixed up, it's just kidney stones.'

'I kept saying to myself that I'd look a right idiot when I have to tell people it's not cancer.' She takes a quiet sip of tea. 'But I know that it is.'

'And now you have to take great care of yourself and be totally honest with me and Rob.' Mum has always had a habit of not telling us when she's poorly, quite often we'd find out months later if at all. It was ok when Dad was alive, he was there to take care of her, but now she's on her own.

Dad was a totally different kettle of fish; he was at the doctors every week with some ailment or other, but it still took them years to diagnose his dementia and only because a young locum saw him that day and referred him to the memory clinic.

'I will.' I look at her. 'I promise.'

'You're only fooling yourself in the end, Mum,' I begin with my speech. 'If the pain gets bad again, then you'll have to go in for stronger pain relief. If you need to sleep, then sleep. There's no gold medal for fighting sleep when you're tired. It's your body's way of fighting the cancer. It puts you to sleep so all it needs to concentrate on is breathing while it tries to figure out what the fuck it's meant to do with a tumour the size of a grapefruit on your kidney.' I rarely use the f word in front of my mum, but this situation really calls for it. 'And I know you don't particularly want to eat, but you've got to. You've lost enough weight already and regardless of what happens after you've got a big operation ahead of you and you need to be as fit and healthy as possible.' Maybe I'm being a bit harsh, I don't know, but she needs to hear this and she needs to hear it now. 'And no trying to come home the day after your operation either. It's just not practical.'

'I know that.' She says softly, and I'm a little taken aback. I thought I was going to have to fight a lot harder than this.

'Hospitals are geared up to help people recover from operations. Everything is on one floor with a bed that goes up and down to help you get comfy and in and out.' I remember when I'd had my c-section, all I wanted to do was get home with my baby but I couldn't even get into bed because it was too low so I ended up sleeping on the sofa for three nights and the burning pain when I had to walk upstairs was so intense it made me cry.

'I'm not going to be silly about it.' She says, and I believe her. 'I'm thinking three to five nights in the hospital, even a week maybe. Just see how I'm feeling.'

'That's the best way to look at it Mum,' I suggest. 'You might feel ok after three nights, or you might still feel like shit after a week. Jade said there's absolutely no rush and you leave when you're ready and not before.'

'Now, what did Mr Martin say about my lungs?' I was hoping she hadn't heard that bit. I don't want her to worry any more than she has to but I'm also not going to lie to her. I remember when Grandad Hunt had his brain tumour, Nan didn't want him to know he was dying. I don't know why. But from diagnosis to death was six weeks, and he never knew. Of course he knew he was ill, but he fought and fought, determined to get better but it was untreatable and without the intervention of medicine, no matter how hard he fought, it was a battle he couldn't win. But in my opinion, he should have been told.

'He said there are some areas of concern in your lungs, little nodules that they're not sure about.' He had tried to show us on the screen.

'You see this light here?' He had circled it with his pen. 'Watch how it doesn't move. It's like a flashlight going on and off. The other bits move away, that's fine, but these stay exactly where they are.'

'So it has spread.' I shake my head.

'The truth is Mum, they don't know.' And this is the truth. 'He said, for now, they're concentrating on getting the tumour and the kidney out so you can recover from that and then they'll re-examine the lungs.' Unfortunately, it's quite common for kidney cancer to spread to the lungs. I think there's a vein or something that connects them.

She nods and asks for some toast. I make a few slices, spreading butter and jam onto two of them and make more tea.

What is it with the British and making tea? We make tea for good things and for bad. Someone dies, pop the kettle on, someone's born, pop the kettle on, got a problem, let's have a cuppa and a chat. I don't think there's an occasion that we haven't 'popped the kettle on' for?

After almost twenty-four hours of labour with my daughter, the midwife bought me tea and toast and it was like nectar. Like that cup of tea could wash away all the pain from the past day, and it did. A nice cup of tea is magic.

We sit there for a good hour, chatting about nothing in particular, we've said everything that can be said for now, no point going over and over it all. It's just a waiting game, but the worst kind of waiting. Not like when you're waiting for a holiday and it's all excitement, but it's a feeling I can't quite explain. You know it has to happen, that the only possible way Mum can get better is to have this operation, so you want it to come as quickly as it can, but then there's that dread that comes with any operation. Knowing the potential risks but not actually having any real choice in the matter. Of course she could say no, but then she won't get better and will be continually bleeding and in pain, so not having the operation isn't an option.

Rob pops in during the afternoon and I mean 'pops'. He stands in the hallway, peeks in briefly to talk to Mum and then goes again. Like a summer shower. Brief and not remotely refreshing. I know he'll get better; he'll work it out in his own head at some point, but during that time it all falls to me.

After taking Mum to get some shopping and having a McDonalds on the way back, I finally decide it's time to get myself home. There's nothing else I can do now, and we've just got to muddle through as best we can. I've offered to stay but she doesn't want that and to be honest, I don't think it would be a good thing anyway. We do things so differently, and she isn't an invalid. She likes her own space and to do things her way; me being there will probably just wind her up after a few days.

With a hug and 'I love you' from my mum, I'm in the car and driving a way I could probably drive blindfolded. Up the road, past The Burnt Post and the shops, down the highway and round the roundabout where The Harvester is. Many, many Dean family events have been spent in that Harvester over the decades. And then as I turn onto Brown's Lane, for no reason, I cry.

Not a little tear, but a full on, uncontrollable sob. I must pull over because suddenly I can't see and my whole body is racked with the held in weight of my grief. I'm not near anyone's house and everyone will be at work, so I just sit there, outside the old Jaguar plant where Dad worked, which is now an Amazon hub and cry.

There's no reason to why it happened then. I bit like the baby blues I suppose. One minute you're absolutely fine, chatting about the weather and then you're in floods. Perhaps it was being alone, allowing my brain to finally think and take in the news instead of having to be strong for everyone else. But who is there to be strong for me?

Chapter 17

I'm not sure how I made it home, but I did. The house is empty, of course it is. My kids are on holiday, where I should be, but instead, I'm sitting here in the living room, staring into space and wishing I could tell the world to just fuck off. Honestly, what exactly is the point?

You work hard, save hard, well, saving at the minute has gone right out of the window. And for what? To have a two-week holiday once a year if you're lucky. To get cancer or dementia in your early seventies and then shuffle off this mortal coil before you've used the pension you've been paying into for the best part of fifty years.

I know I'm angry. Why shouldn't I be? And for once, I allow myself to be. Not for long but long enough to indulge in a packet of shortbread biscuits, a Harry Potter film and a few blackberry gins before falling asleep on the sofa and waking up with crumbs down my bra, an empty glass on the floor and daylight streaming in from the curtains that are still open because it wasn't dark when I fell asleep.

There's a few messages from concerned friends, but I honestly cannot be arsed at the moment. I ring Mum, she's ok, had a decent sleep and has eaten breakfast. I could just sit here all day and wallow. No one would blame me, but what would it actually achieve? So, I jump in the shower, sing along to my angry play list which includes Kate Nash, Amy

Studt, Olivia Rodrigo and my personal rediscovered favourite after her performance at Glastonbury, Lily Allen's Fuck You! And I don't even care that the window is open, and the neighbours can hear.

I'm feeling human again, so I grab my book, a bottle of water and go outside and sit under my gazebo. It's far too hot to sit in the full sun but I love the garden, so I invested in a pop-up gazebo a few years ago and now I put it up every year and it stays up from May to September.

My phone pings and I glance down, smiling when I recognise the name. I can't believe he messaged me yesterday, or that he's still messaging me now.

How are you feeling this morning? I know it must be awful news to take in. I try not to get involved too much with the patient's families, but as soon as you said your name that way, I just knew it was you.

Having been reading back over my diaries, it's strange to think of him as grown up now, all those hopes and dreams we had. He obviously followed his though, unlike me. I just sort of fell into my job. I'd had no desire to work in accounts and payroll. I like maths so started applying after sixth form and finally ended up with an apprenticeship. Shit pay, long hours plus college, but they paid for my qualifications, and I wouldn't be here now without them.

I don't know how you do your job, telling people day in and day out that they have cancer. It must be so hard.

It can be, but I just tell myself that even though I'm delivering bad news, I'm giving them good news too.

Thankfully, if they're seeing me, then it's because they have the option of surgery. Of course, sometimes it doesn't work and I have to tell them afterwards. There's a pause and the bubble icon flickers. *I shouldn't have really said that to you, should I?* (facepalm emoji)

(Laughing emoji) *It's ok. We're not stupid, we know the risks and the potential that once you get inside, it might not be as easy as it first appears.*

The nature of the beast, I'm afraid. I've got something to show you. The bubble flickers again before a photo of him comes through. I instantly recognise the place even though he's written 'Our spot' on the caption that accompanied it.

A forty something man, wearing sunglasses and a baseball cap is smiling at the camera, sitting on a sun lounger by the pool at Littlesea. It is undoubtedly Joey.

Oh wow! Then I send him one back of me doing the same. *Mum and Dad took the plunge and bought a caravan on the site with Dad's retirement money, so we go all the time.*

Can you believe it's been over thirty years?

I can and I can't both at the same time. Time is such a funny thing. It seems to go so slowly as a child, a day felt like a year, the six-week school summer holiday a lifetime, but now, now time flies by in the blink of an eye.

We were just innocent fourteen-year-olds. I remember then that I brought the box of diaries home and run inside to fetch them, taking a screenshot of the polaroid from 1990. *Look what I found yesterday.*

You were my first kiss. Well, my first proper kiss. I can imagine him laughing as he types this, perhaps a little embarrassed to admit it to me.

And you were mine. I didn't know I was his it at the time. *I thought you were far more experienced than me.*

I just winged it. I wanted to impress you.

Well, you did.

Do you remember our pact?

I could lie and say yes, but do I honestly think he has?

Sometimes it clicks what the date is.

Same here. I did the first two years, but then it kind of slipped out of my memory. I see you have children now.

The conversation continued for a while, general chit chat and what we've been up to all these years. Then he asks me a question. A question about a dream that has recently resurfaced.

Did you ever become a writer?

I am absolutely amazed that he remembered this. A childhood dream of mine that I never fulfilled. It seemed such a daft thing as I grew older. Why would anyone want to read something I'd written? I wasn't capable of writing anything as good as the books I read. So I put it away in a box in my head, along with all my other dreams and concentrated on bringing up my children. But Joey asking me that question has opened that box wide open and suddenly it's something I'm desperate to do.

No.

Why?

Never found the time.

You need to make the time. There's one thing I've learnt from my job and that's life chucks curveballs at you and if you don't make time for your dreams, one day, time will run out on you.

That's rather profound for a weekday afternoon.

True though.

I can feel a kind of sadness in his tone. As if being a surgeon was somehow someone else's dream. I can't remember if he told me anything. I recall football and computer games, but wasn't that every teenage boy's dream?

We grow up though, don't we?

Doesn't mean we have to grow old.

I ponder on his words for the rest of the day. Why does growing up mean we have to grow old? Why should childhood dreams be pushed aside just because we have children and mortgages? Surely there are people out there who follow their own dreams and help their children to follow theirs?

In complete contrast to last night's sleep, I feel like I've been awake for most of it. It's been like this for a while now. Blame the menopause. I fall asleep absolutely fine, then after a few hours I need a wee, and then that's it. I even wake up just to turn over and don't get me started on night sweats.

One minute, lovely and comfortable, snuggling under the duvet, and the next I'm throwing it off and reaching for the fan, even in the middle of winter. I used to love fluffy pyjamas, but these days it's a short, cotton shirt which I often change halfway through the night.

The best way to describe it is like someone switching on a furnace inside and ramping it up to the highest heat and leaving it running. Then remembering to come back and switch it off just as quickly as it came on. Similar to the hot flush, but it's the randomness of hot flushes I think that catches you off guard the most.

Everyone knows about night sweats and hot flushes. I can remember my mum standing in front of the fridge on many an occasion, but the brain fog, lack of motivation and the mood swings are so draining.

I think that's the best way to describe it. In this week's TikTok, Davina McCall described the symptoms of menopause as debilitating and she is so right. She's been an amazing advocate for menopause and perimenopause. I've been trying to get help with my symptoms for over two years but with Covid and being under forty-five it's been difficult, but Davina gave me the confidence to stand my ground and I finally got HRT late last year.

I can honestly say I'm a new woman, no, not a new woman, that's wrong. I'm me, the same me, but finally the old me. The one with energy and get up and go. The one that could remember why she went upstairs and didn't put the shopping away in the washing machine rather than the fridge.

But tonight it's not the menopause keeping me awake. It's a story, no, not a story, it's characters. Two people who met in childhood and reconnect as adults. They won't shut up, so I switch on the light and search for a notepad and pen, finding one of the children's old schoolbooks in the junk drawer downstairs.

Finding a working pen is another adventure and eventually I remember the new ones I got last year when I was writing Christmas cards.

Sitting on the sofa, I pause. I have absolutely no idea where to start. Do I literally start? Write down a first line and work from there. Or do I make a plan for what I want to happen? Seeing as I have absolutely no idea what's going to happen, I decide on just writing the first line and taking it from there.

Before I know it, five hours have passed and I'm three chapters in and desperate to write more, but my hand is aching. I've not written this much since A Levels. I need a laptop. The children have them and I've got a computer at work, but I would like one of my own so that I can write anywhere. I quite fancy sitting in a coffee shop typing away like I'm famous or something.

After making a cup of tea, I browse Argos online. As I've no idea what size I need, I look at the children's ones. I then make an informed decision based on this, my budget and stock availability in my local store.

I'm so excited all of a sudden that I'm halfway to Argos before I realise that I've still got my slippers on and now I face the dilemma of driving home to change or just walking in and hoping no one notices. They are just grey boots, fluffy obviously, but I decide that if I just walk in, head held high, I'll get away with it. And in all honesty, who's going to say anything, anyway? I've seen people in full night attire in shops before. Yes, my brain has thought that's a little odd, but I've never gone up and said anything to them. It's absolutely none of my business what other people do or don't do. The world would be a much better place if everyone thought that and stopped being so judgemental.

I chat with Mum for a while on the phone while the laptop loads, updates, whatever it is that it needs to do and then I start typing up the chapters I've handwritten into Word. I'm not the fastest at typing, but I used to practise with Mum's old secretary books when I was a teenager, so I'm not too bad.

Then I'm ready for fresh words and it feels so exciting to be creating this whole world, this story for these two characters. Before I know it, I'm back in the 1990s once again.

Chapter 18

'Don't you have homework?' Mum asks as I walk down the stairs on Saturday morning after announcing at breakfast that I'm spending the day with Christian.

'We're doing it together at his dad's house.' Mum purses her lips. I know she wants to tell me I can't go, she's desperate to, but because I have my school bag and have announced my intentions, there isn't really a lot she can say. 'I'm having tea there too.' If she purses her lips anymore, I think they'll disappear completely. 'And then Christian will drop me home this evening sometime.' I don't have curfews as such at weekends and holidays.

Dad is at work as he usually is on a Saturday. Rob is still asleep, so it's just me and Mum. It's not like we'd be doing anything together, she normally does the food shopping with Nan and I'll either go into town with the girls or watch Saturday morning TV although that's not the same since Going Live finished in April.

'You can invite him here, you know.' I know I can, but honestly, I'm not ready to subject him to my family just yet. Plus, where are we supposed to go? I have the smallest room in the house, with only a bed that we can sit on. We don't have a separate dining room and I'm not about to sit in the living room watching Noel's House Party with my family and Christian. Although I do find it hilarious. 'Just be safe.'

And by that she means everything from putting on my seatbelt in the car to using a condom if we have sex. Now, obviously, we aren't anywhere near that stage, and I hope my mum knows this, but I know she is hinting at it for the future.

'I'm always safe Mum, you know that.' It's true, I am. I'm the sensible one of her children. The one who always says where she's off to and is always exactly where she said she'd be. Well, except for the odd little white lie like the other day at The Milk Bar. But never over anything big or potentially dangerous.

A knock on the door makes me nervous. Shit, he's early. Mum is close to the door and I see a little look of triumph in her eyes. I panic. There's no way I can get to the front door before her and she knows it.

'Hello there.' She's opened the door and I'm still halfway down the stairs. 'You must be Christian? Won't you come in?' I run down the last few stairs.

'Erm…' I can hear how nervous he is just from that one little sound. I've probably painted my mum out to be a right battle axe and he's probably scared half to death of her before he's even met her. She's a good mum really, one of the best, if I'm honest. She just gets a little protective, that's all. 'I've left the engine running.'

I watch as Mum puts her head out the door to check if this, is in fact, true. Thankfully, it is.

'Well, why don't you come for Sunday dinner tomorrow then?' This has thrown me completely and utterly off guard.

'That would be lovely, thank you.' I'm standing behind my mother now, eager to be off.

'Shall we say one o' clock?' He nods. 'I'll let you two go, then. Don't work too hard, it is Saturday after all.' And with a cheery wave she starts humming to herself and walks back into the kitchen.

'What did you do to my mum?' I ask him as he shifts the car into first gear and heads off down the road. 'She was happy and smiling and humming.'

'Must be the Sawyer charm.' He laughs.

'Well whatever it is, you obviously made a good first impression.' I can see that he is dressed quite conservatively. Non-ripped jeans and a plain white long-sleeved shirt. 'She's never asked any of my boyfriends to Sunday dinner before.'

'And have there been many of these?' He asks jokingly, but I can tell there's a small hint of jealousy underneath.

'Nobody serious.' This is true. The longest relationship I've been in was two weeks over the Christmas holiday with a boy in my class called John. This was when I was fifteen and I haven't had a boyfriend since. 'You?' Of course, I know about the girl he almost slept with.

'Only Mandy last year.' Hearing her name on his lips gives me a little stab in the heart. This is even though I know he has absolutely no feelings for her whatsoever and their relationship is long over, it still hurts a little to think of him with other girls. Daft, isn't it? He didn't even know me then.

'Could we pop to the library before going to your dad's house?' I ask, remembering just in time that he will need to turn right at the lights and not left. 'I need to take my books back and get some new ones.' I've finished Wideacre, and it was an absolute delight, so I'm hoping they will have the next one in the series, The Favoured Child.

'If you want, but you'll have to tell me how to get there.' I direct him as we go down past our school and then into one of the little cul-de-sacs. It's a strange place to have a library. The houses are all around the outside in a circle and then in the middle is a small hill with a large, one room building plonked on the top. It reminds me of my old primary school classrooms. Large windows and high walls with a sloping roof.

'Are you coming in?' I ask after he's pulled into one of the small bays. I usually walk or cycle.

'Why not?' He says, turning off the engine and rushing round to open the door for me.

'You don't have to keep doing that, you know.' I like that he does it but it really isn't necessary.

'I like to.' He follows me through the sliding door, and I'm immediately hit with the familiar smell of dust and books. It's a smell unlike any other and a smell that brings me such joy and peace. I'm sure it's distinctive to this library because Central Library in the city centre isn't the same. Earlsdon was similar when I went there with Mum to pick up a Catherine Cookson book she was after, so I'm thinking it's due to the small, older buildings rather than the large, modern one in the town.

But there is something totally unique to Finham Library and I'm instantly transported to my childhood as I walk in.

I return my books to the lady behind the huge counter, and she scans them in. I still remember the days when there was a card at the front of the book in a little pouch. The library hasn't really changed over the years. The children's section is in one corner with picture books in open wooden cubes and then around the edges on shelves are the books for older children. I lost count of the times I checked out The Famous Five Adventures.

The teen section is kind of in the middle and this is where I fell in love with historical romance books. A Savage Spirit by Meg Cameron. Just delightful. I think I kept it for about three years and read it over and over.

Then there is adult fiction and nonfiction. Split into relevant genres. Mum loves Catherine Cookson, but she's also partial to Jilly Cooper. She let me watch the TV adaptation of Riders with her when it was on earlier this year. I already had a crush on Michael Praed from Robin of Sherwood, but he was just lovely as Jake.

Dad uses the library usually for car manuals, sometimes for Bernard Cornwell's Sharpe series or the odd Bond novel. Whenever he gets a new car, which is quite often because he's a mechanic and loves to tinker with engines, he'll pop down to the library and borrow the Haynes guide. There's hundreds of them. He then renews them over and over again and heaven help anyone that reserves it, he reserves it straight back.

'Anything you fancy?' I'm searching for Gregory, but no luck and he's looking in the sci-fi section.

'I've heard of this.' He shows me a Terry Pratchett book.

'The Discworld series?' He nods. 'Meant to be really good. I'll check it out for you if you want.' He nods and hands me the book and I find another five to take me to my six-book limit.

'Ready?' He watches me put the books in my bag and we head back to the car.

It's only twenty minutes to Walsgrave and we pull up outside a very ordinary-looking house.

'Oh.'

'You sound disappointed.' He parks on the drive and again rushes round to open the door and this time I don't question him about it.

'No, it's just...well...not what I was expecting.' I don't know what I was expecting but the way he's talked about his dad these past few days, you would have thought he owned a mansion.

'Were you expecting a castle or something?' He laughs, locking the car door before turning the key in the front door. 'Hi Dad.' He calls as we walk in. I'm immediately struck by how modern everything is inside. It's in complete contrast to the thirties exterior. 'See.'

Now I know what he means. As we walk through the living room, there is every conceivable item of entertainment. A huge TV, speakers on the wall, a double video recorder, games consoles and the biggest Hi-Fi stack I've ever seen. The kitchen is just as bedecked with modern appliances, a coffee maker, microwave, oven and even a Soda Stream. It's also three times the size of mine at home with a breakfast bar and high-backed stools.

'Wow.' Is all I can think of to say.

'Dad?' He calls again after opening the back door.

'Here Son,' comes the reply and we walk into the garden. It's huge and I can now see that the original house has been extended. There's even a building at the bottom that an older, grey-haired version of Christian is walking out of. He comes up the path towards us, his arm outstretched and a welcoming smile on his face. 'And this must be Charlie that I've been hearing so much about.' I shake his hand and am pleased to see a slight look of embarrassment on Christian's face. 'I'm Tony.'

'It's a pleasure to meet you.' I say. 'You have a lovely house.'

'It's ok.' He says, waving away my compliment. 'Just trying to fix the pool filter.'

Did I hear correctly? Pool? It's then that I notice the building is made almost entirely of glass, currently with blinds down.

'You have a pool?' My mouth drops open in shock and I quickly close it, so I don't look like a fish. 'In your garden?' This is beyond luxury to me. Only rich people have pools in their gardens.

'Dad built it.' Christian says proudly, and I can see that he has a lot of love and respect for his dad.

'Then I'm doubly impressed.' Christian takes my hand and leads me inside after his dad has announced making us a drink and heading back into the kitchen.

The smell of chlorine hits you instantly.

'Once it's fixed we can have a swim.' He says as we walk round the sides before stopping at the end. 'I'd love to see you in a swimsuit.' The way he's looking at me right now makes my knees go weak. I've read about these feelings in romance novels but thought they must be nonsense, but right now I feel like my skin is on fire.

His eyes are looking at me as if he wants to eat me, as if he's a wolf and I'm his prey. Dear God, do I want to be his prey? There's a weird feeling between my legs. I've no idea what it is, I've never felt it before, but suddenly I want to grab him, push him up against the wall and kiss him and take his shirt off and…

'Here we go then.' I jump a little as Tony comes back into the room and we all sit on the sun loungers drinking Coke and making small talk and all the while I'm looking at Christian and he's looking at me and it's as if he knows exactly what I've just been imagining, because it's mirrored in his eyes.

Chapter 19

The day passes in a blur of visitors. Tony's friends come by on their way back from town and join us for lunch. It's such a nice day that we eat outside on the patio. Then, after they've gone, Christian's Uncle Lou arrives with a video tape of some new show he's recorded on his satellite TV, The X Files or something. He thinks Christian will like it. Apparently, it's about searching for aliens. He promises he'll watch it, but I'm not sure, sounds a bit daft to me.

Tony's mum arrives just before five and brings us homemade lasagne and apple pie before whisking Tony off to visit another uncle in hospital. Finally, we're alone.

We're sitting on the sofa downstairs, the TV is on, Jim Davidson's Big Break is about halfway through.

'I think Back to the Future Two is on after this.' He says, picking up the Radio Times. 'Or we could watch that show Uncle Lou recorded.' I shrug. 'Or a film?' He senses I'm not really interested in any of these things. 'What's wrong?'

'Nothing.' How can I tell him what's going on in my head? All these strange feelings and weird sensations are churning me up inside, and I don't know what to do about them. We had a very limited sex talk at school in third year. We were shown an illustrated version of how a woman gets pregnant, followed by a video of an actual baby being born. Poor India fainted at this, right off the science stool and onto the floor.

Luckily, she fell backwards and not forwards otherwise she'd have smashed her face on the work bench. Then the boys got taken away, and we were shown how to use tampons and sanitary towels and given free samples.

But no one talks about how it actually feels. How when you meet someone, your body wants to do all sorts of random things with them that you'd never think to do otherwise. For example, why would you want to stick your tongue in someone else's mouth and what possesses anyone to want a boy's thingy in their private parts? It's as if my body knows exactly what it wants to do and how to do it though. I've never seen a man's penis in real life and the girls and I always used to giggle about how odd it looked in books. Lyn and India have already had sex with their boyfriends. They're eighteen in a few weeks, though, and felt ready. Up until this moment, I've felt far from ready.

Then, of course, there's being accused of acting like a slag. Girls are told over and over again not to have sex unless you're in a long-term relationship. Only girls with no morals sleep around but boys get slapped on the back for it. Such a double standard.

And again, no one talks about feelings. How at this very moment in time I want to jump on Christian and rip his clothes off? But it makes me feel so guilty because I've been told time and time again how wrong it is when I've only known him for a few days and I feel sure I must be blushing because he's looking at me so strangely.

'Tell me.' He says softly, sidling up the sofa so we are next to each other. His leg touches mine. This has not helped the situation. 'You can tell me anything at all, Charlie. I won't ever laugh at you or judge you.' He takes hold of my hand in his and turns slightly so he's looking at me. He looks so sincere and honest. And that's another thing.

What if the guys only want one thing?

Something else we are warned about. Boys only wanted to cop off with girls or have sex with them if they could before boasting and bragging about it to their mates. This is followed by said girl having a bad reputation and the boy being a bloody hero. Life isn't fair.

It's not the same with Christian though. I know he's popular, but he seems different somehow, more sensitive.

'I don't know how to say it?' He doesn't seem to understand what I'm trying to say to start with. 'You know?' He shakes his head and looks at me with a puzzled expression. 'When we were by the pool earlier.'

It's like a light bulb went off in his head at that precise moment and he raises his eyebrows at me in an extremely sexy way.

'You mean you want to talk about sex, right?' He nods as though the subject is exactly what he wants to discuss as well.

'Not talk about it exactly.' This statement has definitely caught him off guard, and I can see he's really unsure about what to do or say next.

'You mean you want to have sex?' He says sex this time in a totally different way. It's almost as if he's saying a swear word in front of an adult. 'Like, now?'

'No…Yes…I mean…God! I don't know what I mean.' He relaxes a little.

'Just try and tell me.' He kisses me on the lips, a small reassuring kiss. 'Or show me if you think that's easier.' I honestly don't know if I can actually tell him all these things that are going on in my head and in my body, but how can I show him?

'I don't know what to do.' I say, feeling every inch the virgin that I am. And I know he is too, but he seems much more worldly than me.

'Do whatever you want to do.' He kisses me again, and this time it's filled with passion and longing. I respond instantly, my body knowing instinctively what to do. My hands weave into his hair, pulling him closer to me and I arch my chest towards him so we can be touching in as many places as possible.

His lips leave my mouth and travel down my jawline, onto my neck and down. He undoes the buttons on my shirt so he can kiss the top of my boobs. I don't know what to do with myself. Every kiss leaves my skin tingling and wanting more. Before I know it my shirt is undone and he's reaching round to unclasp my bra. Oh Jesus! Is this what I want?

He senses my hesitation and stops immediately. Kissing me on the nose, he lies down on the sofa and pulls me beside him. His breathing is ragged, as if he's just run round the block.

'I'm sorry.' I genuinely am. I don't want him to think I'm a tease.

'What is there to be sorry about?' He asks, cuddling me into the side of him so my face is on his chest. I can feel my nipples brushing against him through the thin shirt he has on and this causes that weird feeling between my thighs once again.

'Why does it make me feel funny?' I ask, not realising what I've said until I've said it.

'Why does what make you feel funny?' He kind of looks down at me.

'When we kiss.' I can't look at him so I speak into his chest. 'Or just now when my boobs brushed against you.' My face is on fire. I can't believe I'm saying this to anyone, let alone a boy.

'Where does it make you feel funny?' He places his hand on my heart. 'Here?'

'A little.' It makes my heart flutter when he kisses me.

'Here?' He touches his palm to my stomach.

'Yes.' I whisper, my insides churning because I'm pretty sure I know what's coming next.

'Or here.' And with the final here he has cupped me gently between my thighs. Although there's a pair of pants and thick denim jeans in the way, it's as if he's touching my bare skin and I suddenly want to cry out and wiggle against him. I can feel his smile rather than see it and he moves his hand away. 'Another time.' He says and I feel strangely disappointed as well as annoyed and frustrated. 'That, Charlie my love, is called lust.'

'Lust?' I know what lust is, but I've always thought it was quite a horrible word, people lusting over other people or things.

'Lust has kept the human race going for millions of years.' He takes my hand again and places it on his chest, leaving his own on top.

'Surely you mean, love?' He shakes his head.

'It's not love that makes you want to have sex.' I think I disagree with this statement, but he continues before I have a chance to say anything. 'Don't get me wrong, people make love, people that are in love have sex etc…but honestly, it's lust that makes you crave sex in the first place. It's that attraction, that carnal desire, that base human instinct that makes us want to jump into bed with someone.' I think I understand what he's saying.

'Like when you get told beauty is only skin deep and you shouldn't judge a book by its cover?' I lean on my elbows to look up at him.

'Exactly.' He agreed with me. 'If you didn't fancy me, would you be here now?'

'What makes you think I fancy you?' I can't have him getting a big head.

'Because when I do this.' He kisses me hard and quick and it takes my breath away for a moment. 'Or this.' He kisses me again, so softly that it's barely there, but I can feel myself pushing against him, wanting to be as close to him as possible. 'You do that.' His breathing has become ragged again, and he looks a little out of sorts. 'You don't know what you do to me.' He whispers into my hair.

I feel empowered by his sudden show of weakness. No, weakness isn't the word. Oh, how to explain it?

'Show me.' I say, suddenly feeling confident and extremely bold.

He takes my hand and places it on his crotch. I can feel something stiff and large under his jeans.

'That's what you do to me.' He kisses me again, and as he does, I can feel his penis pulsating under my hand. 'Shit!' He suddenly sits up and starts brushing his hand through his hair. 'Dad's home.'

I panic as I hear a car door and voices outside getting closer as their owners near the door. We both fumble with my buttons, doing them up as quickly as possible, then arranging ourselves on the sofa to look as innocent as possible. Christian has had to pull his shirt down and this makes me laugh. At least no one can see when a girl is aroused.

'Your Uncle Tom fell asleep after five minutes.' Christian's nan announces as she walks into the living room. 'So we thought we might as well come home.'

'What have you two been up to?' Tony asks and I'm sure he knows exactly what we've been doing.

'Just watching a film.' Luckily BBC One is still on and currently Marty McFly is driving a flying DeLorean.

'Good is it?'

'Brilliant.'

'I like this one, the third one, the flying train at the end, sheer brilliance.'

'Yeah, it's good that bit.'

'This is number two, Son.' And with that he pats Christian on the shoulder and it's only when we're driving home that I realise my shirt is buttoned up completely wrong.

Chapter 20

My phone ringing wakes me up and I realise I've fallen asleep on the sofa again. The laptop is open, although it has switched itself off. I press the mouse quickly, panicking in case any of my work has been lost or I've accidentally erased everything by pressing the delete button. I sigh in relief when I realise it's all there and I save it to my computer, USB stick and email it to myself too.

After losing a report I'd spent three days on, backing up is something I do regularly now.

'Hi Sweetheart, everything ok?' It's my eldest, announcing that they've landed and are waiting for customs and baggage collection. 'I'll be outside arrivals. See you in a bit, love you.'

It's an effort to move quickly these days, what with being hypermobile. This is a recent discovery on the female side of the family after my daughter dislocated her knee twice in three years. We all thought we were just extra bendy. I can still touch my toes, even with the extra weight I carry and I know now it's because my knee joint bends inwards as well as outwards and the fact that Mum regularly pops her knee back in is not something regular people have to do.

My daughter has an official diagnosis and now requires additional support for university and future work. She tires so easily and suffers with pain in her fingers when writing, so is given extra time to write notes etc…she definitely has it the worst of all of us. I think the doctor said it's in seven of the eight joints. Mine is just wrists and knees, but the pain it causes in my lower legs is unbearable at times. Coupled with menopause and general aging, it's becoming a bit of a nightmare but there's not a lot I can do about it apart from general exercises and painkillers, so I just get on with it the best way I can.

I make a hands-free call to Mum on the way to the airport. There's still three weeks to go till her operation and I can tell it's getting her down and she's getting maudlin about things. For example…

Mum: *You're better at these things than me. Is there a version of Cliff singing Softly as I leave you that doesn't have people clapping on it?*

Me: *I don't think so. I'm sure he's only ever released a live version.*

Mum: Thought so.

That was it for a few minutes until…

Mum: *I'm struggling to find my funeral songs.* **:D :D :D**

I'm sure she thinks she's being funny using laughing emojis, but honestly, I don't find it amusing at all. I get it, I really do. She's seventy-four, diagnosed with cancer and having a rather large operation soon, but sitting planning your funeral? Really? And then tell your daughter about it? It's also one of the songs we played at Dad's funeral, not Cliff's version, but Matt Monro. It was the perfect song, to be honest. It played as we walked out and just as Mum, Rob and

I had said our final goodbye to him and were leaving the room, the last line…as I leave you there…rang out.

She's a little more upbeat this morning, thankfully. She's had an online delivery from Ocado, telling me how good it is and how she got free delivery and fifteen pounds off and then, in the next breath, telling me she'll probably use Morrisons next time. I do despair of her sometimes, I really do. There is absolutely no logic to her in the slightest.

'Me and the kids will pop over and see you tomorrow, Mum.' I say as I pull into the arrival parking at Birmingham Airport. 'Best go, I can see them.' Luckily, they are just walking out of the door as I arrive, so I don't have to pay for parking. They all look gloriously suntanned, happy and smiling.

Kisses and hugs are hurried as we load the bags into the car and then off home, dropping my son's friend off who took my place at the last minute on the way. It's so lovely to be in a car filled with chatter once again, although later on when I'm on my fifth load of washing, I may feel differently.

They ask about their nan, of course, and the motherly instinct to protect them kicks in. I dumb down her symptoms and the potential risks as much as I can. I don't even mention the issue with her lungs or the worrying cough she has now developed. No need for them to worry as well as me. After early flights, they're all tired so it's off to bed and I can finally grab some breakfast and a cup of tea.

There is a message in the group chat from Claire announcing engagement drinks in London in November. After swearing she would never get married, she's finally found the one that she wants to spend the rest of her life with and I couldn't be more thrilled for her. I'm so excited to have a close friend getting married again. It's been decades since I have been to a wedding because I wanted to rather than because I had to.

You know what I mean…family weddings…you go because you have to go. It's like a written law or something. You don't see these people from one year to the next but if there's a wedding, engagement, or big birthday party, its obligatory that extended family get invited.

As much as I would love to say, yes, I can't. Therefore, it's the answer that has become my standard reply to any invite from anyone that involves any occasion for the rest of the year. *It depends on Mum.*

And it does, because, let's face it, best case scenario, she makes a full recovery and needs no further treatment, she's still not going to be fully fit till, say, mid-October. Middle case scenario she needs further treatment, you'll be talking end of the year, early next year and I'm not even considering the worst case. I push it right out of my head before it even has time to take the tiniest hold in my brain. That's a slippery slope I don't want to go down unless I absolutely bloody well have to.

I head back to my book. It's really taking shape now and I'm amazed at how the words are flowing. It's just pouring out of me and I wish I'd done this sooner, but then, I didn't have the full story before Joey messaged.

Talking of Joey, we've chatted most nights. He's asked to meet up for a drink, but I don't feel it's the right time. He's Mum's surgeon and in three weeks he'll be cutting her open and removing the tumour and her kidney and I just know that if I was to meet him now, this side of the operation, I'll be asking him all sorts of questions. This is not fair to him or me. I go to type things to him but delete them when I remember and quite often end up putting something daft instead. He must think I've turned into a right wally.

I find myself saying all kinds of things to him and him to me, quite personal details about relationships and stuff and I find it odd that we have such a close connection. It's a bit like when there was a primary school reunion a few years ago. One of our classmates took his own life, and it brought us all together again on Facebook and a few of us met up. You spent day after day with these people for the best part of seven years, some twelve and even fourteen years and even if you weren't best friends at school, you just felt bonded with them because of the joint experiences you shared.

School sports days, ringing the bell for breaktime, milk in a carton that was always warm because no one refrigerated it after it had been delivered or running down the dell. Health and safety would have a field day with that now. The books, Roger Red Hat, Billy Blue Hat and Jennifer Yellow Hat. Why was she Jennifer Yellow Hat? Couldn't she have been Ginny Green Hat? The sick bed outside the nurse's office that you used to lie in if your mum or dad couldn't pick you up when you were feeling poorly. The huge TV that got wheeled in so you could watch Words and Pictures and sing The Magic E song or one of the shows like Dark Towers or Kez.

Even though Joey and I only spent a week together back when we were fourteen, it was virtually twenty-four hours a day. Even when we'd gone to bed, my bedroom was opposite his and there wasn't much distance between the two caravans so we used to send notes to each other on a little pulley system he'd rigged up on Sunday night after my mum had told us to stop talking. There's always something special about a bond formed in childhood.

I have absolutely no idea what to do with the book when I'm finished. I've got no clue if it's any good or if anyone will even want to read it. Why would they? But it feels special. Might only be special to me. Then an idea forms.

Would you do me a favour? I ask Joey and then wait for his answer.

Of course. Comes the reply.

Remember you asked if I'd ever written that book, and I said no? Well, I've kind of started writing one and I'd really like an honest opinion on it. I don't want any fluff or beating about the bush, just Charlie its good or Charlie its shit.

Send it to my email.

And that's what I do without hesitation because I know he will give me an honest opinion. I could have shared it with my friends, of course, but I'm not sure if deep down they would tell me what their true feelings were. I can't say I blame them. I'm not sure I could tell them the entire truth if it was the other way round. I'd probably try and be diplomatic about it, like it's not really my thing or something like that.

Then suddenly, doubts hit me and my brain blocks. What if it is shit? What if I'm just wasting my time on some pipe dream? After all, who wants to read the ramblings of a middle-aged, overweight office manager?

I slam the laptop down, not even caring if I've saved my work or not. What does it matter now, anyway?

Deciding to take a bath, I head upstairs and start running the water, adding a bath bomb from The Body Shop. The smell takes me back to my teenage years where we all wore White Musk or Dewberry and gave each other those fruit shaped soaps and squishy scented bath balls for Christmas.

My diary sits next to my bed and I take it into the bathroom with me. The kids won't be up for hours yet, so I can enjoy a really long soak before I need to even think about tea. Maybe we'll get pizza or Chinese instead. Turning the page to where I left off, I smile, a little knowing smile because I can remember what happened on Sunday the 12th of September 1993, even now and in every minute detail.

Chapter 21

My dreams last night were so vivid and sensual that I woke up in hot sweats more times than I care to remember. I hope to God that I didn't call out Christian's name at all. Very unusually, the dream continued each time I fell back to sleep and when I woke up far too early for a Sunday; it was just as Christian had laid me on a soft bed. I had no idea where we were, but he was kissing me and telling me how beautiful I was.

We don't have a shower in our house, so it's a cool bath before breakfast. Mum looks at me strangely as I come downstairs because I usually bathe at night. It's not even seven thirty, but she's already prepared the vegetables for lunch and they now sit in three different saucepans on top of the cooker. Thankfully, she's decided to cook beef, not chicken and when I open the fridge to get the milk for my Rice Krispies, there is Yorkshire pudding batter settling and the trifle dish is making an unexpected appearance outside of Christmas and Easter Sunday. I spy the Birds custard and dream topping sachets waiting for when the jelly has cooled. The sprinkles have been put back in the cupboard though because Mum always uses a crushed-up Flake instead.

'Did you get all your homework done?' She asks and I'm momentarily thrown off guard until I remember that's what I said we'd be doing.

'Just got a history essay to do this morning.' This isn't a lie, but it isn't the answer to her question either. Mum doesn't seem to notice and just nods her head in satisfaction.

I take my bowl into the living room, saying hello to Dad who is getting himself ready to go to Nan and Grandad's house for his weekly visit. I switch on the TV and although I'm far too old for cartoons; I watch Pigeon Street and find myself knowing every word of the theme song. Playdays is taking it a little too far though, so I switch it off, make a cup of tea for me and Mum, then wash up the bits in the sink.

'Looks a bit black over Bill's mother's.' She says and I agree, looking at the ominous grey clouds rolling in. Strange saying that isn't it? I mean, why Bill's mum? Was she some poor woman who lived in a house where it rained all the time? Why not Bob's mother? But then Bob's your uncle, isn't he? Stupid sayings.

'Do you need a hand with anything?' I know she'll say no, she always does, regardless of whether there is anything to actually be done. Mum likes to do things her own way and if it's not done her way, then either something ends up ruined or she'll redo the job after we've done it so she thinks she may as well do it herself in the first place. I've vowed never to be like that with my family when I'm older.

And there is that assumption that one day I will be older, married, with a house and family of my own. I've no idea if that's the case. I mean, of course I've started fantasising about Christian and me being together, but it's not even been a week yet, who knows what will happen. We might not be together forever; chances are we probably won't and that makes me feel quite sad.

'Will you just pop round and check on your nan and grandad for me, please?' Now this is a job I am allowed to do. 'Grandad wasn't feeling too well yesterday so if he's no better, we'll have to think about getting the doctor out.'

I head out the back door, through the gate, one step through the entry that sits between the two houses and then through their back gate and into the back door. I love being able to do this. I adore my grandparents, both sets, but Dad's live further away and are a lot older than Mum's. Plus Dad was an only child so there are no cousins on that side, but Mum's side more than makes up for that.

Christmas is a riotous affair with sixteen of us crammed in two rooms, balancing on sofa arms, sitting at picnic tables, but that just makes it so much more fun. I've never known a quiet Christmas. Boxing Day is much more subdued at Dad's parents, just the six of us round their tiny table and although it's not as much fun, I love it just the same.

'Hi Nan.' My Nan is in the kitchen, and like Mum, she has pans of vegetables already prepared for lunch. 'How's Grandad?' I sneak a piece of raw carrot.

'He's not too good, I'm afraid.' I can see that she's worried and that worries me instantly. Nan rarely shows emotion. 'I've just made him a cuppa if you want to take it up to him.'

'No problem.' I grab the 'Who shot JR?' mug and head up the stairs. I always find it strange being in this house. The layout is a perfect mirror image of mine. 'Hi Grandad.' I say softly as I peek into the room, just in case he's asleep. He is, so I leave the cup next to him and head back down the stairs, reporting my findings to Nan.

'It's all he's done since Thursday, Charlotte.' Nan shakes her head. 'I'll call the doctor in the morning if he's no better.' I kiss her on the cheek and head back.

The morning drags, I chat to Lyn on the phone before trying to settle to my history essay but it's no good, the assassination of Archduke Franz Ferdinand is no match for the feel of Christian's lips on mine or when he puts his hand on my…

'Charlotte! Christian's here.' Dad calls. I hadn't heard the door knock but then realised Dad had just come back so must have met him on the driveway. Shit! He's early. I'm still in my slobby clothes after my shower and haven't even attempted to get a brush through my hair, so I pretend I haven't heard and sneak into the hallway and up the stairs the front way as they come in the back.

'I'm just getting changed.' I call down the stairs and hastily pull on my black jeans and my red velour top. It's a little much for a normal Sunday at home, but this is no longer a normal Sunday. My hair refuses to play ball, and the brush keeps getting stuck in the back of it so I just wind it into a bun. Lipstick is too obvious, so a shiny lip gloss will have to do.

I can hear Dad and Christian talking about cars as I walk down the stairs, so I know he's worked his charm on Dad already. A sneaky peek into the kitchen sees Mum arranging fresh flowers in the cut glass vase and she's singing again, so

I think he's made a good first impression on her too. He stands up as I walk into the room and I take in his double denim outfit, he looks so good in blue and the thoughts that race through my head are highly inappropriate for having my dad in the room and my mum in the next. And then he smiles at me and I know that I am totally and utterly lost.

I sit on the sofa and Christian sits next to me, but not close enough to be touching. Dad is in his chair and Mum comes back in, placing the vase on the mantelpiece and preening the flowers some more.

'Thank you so much again for the flowers, Christian.' She says, beaming from ear to ear.

'You're very welcome Mrs Dean, it's the least I could do in return for your kind offer of dinner.' I've not heard him speak as eloquently as this before. He doesn't really have an accent. Most of us born and bred in Coventry don't. Except when we go on holiday and then people think we're from Birmingham because it's the only place in the Midlands that people seem to know.

'Can I get you a drink?' She asks, and he replies that he'd love a Coke if it's no trouble and can he help with anything for dinner. I'm trying not to laugh at his overly polite and posh voice. It appears to be working on Mum, so it's all good.

Mum heads back into the kitchen, reappearing a few short seconds later with a perfectly poured Coke and places it on the little nest of tables next to Christian.

'Thank you so much.' He smiles at her.

'Jerry.' Mum says. 'Can you come and check the beef with me, please?'

I look at Dad and then at Mum, quizzical expressions on our faces. Mum doesn't normally need help with the meat. Dad always carves it, he tried to show me how you cut with the grain so the meat is nice and tender, go against the grain and its tough. Coming from a family of butchers, it's something he's always known how to do. But the joint of beef looked exactly the same to me whichever way he turned it, so I just nodded and pretended I understood. It's not like I'll be carving beef in this house anytime soon, so what did it matter?

'Mum?' Rob has just come in the back door from a night at his girlfriends. 'Why is the beef black?' I see the look of horror cross my mum's face and she rushes into the kitchen, my dad following her after a quick smile to Christian and me.

An hour later and we are eating sausage and mash rather than the roast beef dinner mum had planned. The oven had decided at the most inopportune moment to effectively blow up, burning the beef and throwing itself out of action. Shops and takeaways aren't open on Sundays, so Mum had to throw together whatever she could find and whatever she could cook on the hob.

The sausage ratio isn't good. Being a packet of eight, Mum was originally cooking them as toad in the hole in the week but as she's got no oven, Christian and Rob have been given two and a half and me, Mum and Dad have one paltry sausage each. I want to complain but take one look at the embarrassed and stressed look on Mum's face and decide against it.

'Lovely dinner Mum, thank you.' I say instead and am rewarded with a grateful smile.

Luckily, Mum always cooks enough vegetables to feed an army so with the mash and gravy, we are all full, but somehow find room for the trifle. Mum is looking more relaxed now after two glasses of wine and the chat at the table has become livelier. No awkward silences or long pauses.

They ask about Christian and his family, what he plans to do when he finishes sixth form. There's a stab in my heart when I hear him say that he's looking to move away to university. Daft, really I know. It's a year away and we're not even officially a couple, but the thought of him not being around is something I don't want to contemplate.

Ever the proud father, my dad says. 'Charlotte's applying for university too.' He seems to have forgotten this has been practically forced on me and is not through choice.

'I don't really want to go, though.' I say, scraping my bowl for the last of the trifle and resisting the urge to run my finger round it as I would normally do.

'It's not for everyone,' Christian says. 'I wouldn't go if I could get into teaching any other way.' I had no idea that he wanted to be a teacher, but I know he'd be good at it. He has such a way about him that puts people instantly at ease but also a serious side that will stand him in good stead.

'Charlotte hasn't a clue what she wants to do.' I shoot a look at Mum over the table.

'I'm kind of following in my mum's footsteps and my grandfather before her so it was easier.' He takes my hand under the table and squeezes it. 'It's so hard these days to know what to do.' I squeeze his hand back, grateful for his support. He continues chatting to my parents, but I haven't got a clue what he's saying because his hand is currently on my thigh, stroking it through my jeans. If he carries on, I think I might explode.

Chapter 22

Rob and I have washed up, Christian is of course excused from these duties as he's a guest and has been subjected to yet more questions from my parents in the living room. I keep an ear open and they don't seem to be overly personal but I still wash the dishes as fast as possible and wonder if I can apply to appear on Roy Castle's Record Breakers.

'We're going to watch a film in my room.' I announce and grab Christian's hand before anyone can protest. I lead him upstairs, into my room and close the door before leaning up against it and sighing in relief. 'I'm so sorry about all the questions.'

'It's okay.' He says, standing in front of me. My room isn't overly large, it is the box room after all but it's larger than other box rooms I've seen. I've got my bed up against the wall with a shelving unit Dad built at the bottom for my TV and a video player I was given for my sixteenth birthday. What a luxury to have my own TV and video in my room. Then on the other wall is a small dressing table and a chest of drawers. 'I was expecting them.'

He's right in front of me and my heart is starting to thump in my chest. I can feel my palms getting sweaty and I'm grateful he hasn't tried to hold them. Instead, he has placed his hands on the door, either side of my face and is slowly, tantalisingly slowly leaning towards me. He's so close to me now that I can smell Brut aftershave and if I just reached up a little bit our mouths would touch.

There's a smile hovering on his lips and I wonder if he knows what he's doing to me. Do I do the same to him? I blush when I remember yesterday on the couch, and I can't help my eyes from flickering down. He sees exactly what I'm doing and a hovering smile breaks out across his face. I turn my face away so he can't see me blushing, but he places one hand gently on my chin and locks my gaze in his.

'I don't want you to see me blush.' Because I have permanently red cheeks anyway, when I blush, I tend to turn a delightful shade of scarlet.

'I like it when you blush.' He places a kiss behind my ear. 'It means I've got through that slightly stand-offish air you give out to people.' Now he's kissing my neck.

'I am not stand off…' He claims my lips in his and anything I was about to say or even think is erased from my mind.

'I've been wanting to do that since I walked in the door.' He says, stopping to kiss me for a brief second.

'I've been wanting you to do it.' I reply, bringing my hands up his back so I can hold him against me.

'When I saw you in this top I just wanted to...' But he doesn't need to tell me, I can feel what he wants to do from the way he is kissing me and from the bulge I can feel against my stomach. His hand has left my chin now and has found its way under my top. He's cupping my boob over my bra, and it feels like a thousand tiny nerve endings are exploding under his fingers. 'I want you so much.' He whispers against my hair before trailing kisses down my neck.

I want him too, so so much. Like I've never wanted anything before.

My body is screaming out to touch him and to have him touch me. Places I didn't know existed inside me are on fire and I have no idea how to put them out. The more I touch him, the more he touches me, the hotter it gets. Now I know what Mills and Boon mean by flames of desire.

'Christian.' I say his name, almost as a question, but I have no idea what I'm asking but he seems to know and leads my hand to his penis. He just places it there, no pressure on me to do anything so my hand just sort of rests there, but it feels nice and I can tell from the small groan on his lips that he feels the same.

'I need to stop.' He says quietly and steps back from me. Even though it isn't cold, I feel a draft between us. He's running his hands through his hair and I can hear how fast he is breathing.

'Did I do something wrong?' It's clearly my fault and I'm devastated. My whole world collapses.

'Oh God no.' He kisses me gently, framing my face in his hands. 'Don't ever think that.' He leads me to sit on the bed. 'I just need to stop before we go too far. I don't think having sex with your brother across the landing and your parents in the room underneath would be a particularly wise move.'

As if to emphasise this we hear my brother shouting at the video game he is obviously playing and we both laugh.

Comforted by this I hold his hand. 'I thought I'd done something wrong.'

'You could never do anything wrong.' He reassures. 'If it feels right, then do it, if I don't like it I'll say, or if you're not sure, ask me.' He looks in my eyes. 'And I promise to do the same with you.' He kisses me again and we fall back onto the bed but this time we keep our hands firmly above the waist and over our clothes. I can still feel how aroused he's getting though and as I'm feeling the same, I break from the kissing at an opportune moment and rest my head on his chest.

'What are we going to do then?' I ask.

'I'll think of something.' He rests his hand on my shoulder. 'Where are all your posters then?'

'In my wardrobe.' I sigh.

'What?' He gets up and opens the wardrobe door and sure enough pictures of New Kids on The Block, Christian Slater and Take That are blue tacked inside.

I explain to him that having recently had my bedroom decorated, finally in my own choice, dark blue with gold stars, a sun and moon border and sun and moon curtains, I have been forbidden from putting up posters of any kind and have only been allowed a framed one on my wall which he points to.

'That is my signed poster from Take That.' He examines it closely. 'Me and the girls travelled to Leicester last year when they were doing signings in HMV to coincide with their album release, but it got cancelled because of riots in other cities so my mum wrote to them and complained and they sent me that.' I remember the day it came; I was so excited to think Gary and the band had actually touched that piece of paper.

Claire and I were huge Take That fans. My dad had even driven us to The Radio One Roadshow at Alton Towers last summer and he'd just sat in the car park for the whole day. Their minibus drove past us afterwards and we both screamed at Dad to drive faster so he caught them up and Gary waved at us from the back seat. You couldn't mistake his blond spikes that was for sure.

'I didn't take you for a fan of boy bands.' He teases and moves to my CD and record collection. 'Who is Tori Amos?'

'Oh she's brilliant.' I get up and put the CD on and we sit on the bed listening.

'I like her.' He says. 'Very different from Take That though.'

'I don't just like pop you know.' I do get annoyed when people assume you're a certain type of person because of the music you listen to or the way you dress. I know most people think I'm a goth and therefore must listen to that type of music but I'm not and I listen to all sorts. I love Bryan White who's a country singer, Pet Shop Boys, Depeche Mode and even Cliff Richard. It's like my taste in books. I like a story or a song rather than the person who sings it or writes it. Except Take That of course, I just love Take That.

'How about that film then?' He looks through my very limited tape collection, most of which have been recorded off the TV. 'Shall we pop down to the shop and see what they've got?'

At the bottom of the four streets is Sowe Avenue which connects them all and towards the end is a row of shops. We have a hairdresser, a paper shop, a little grocery store which I wasn't allowed to enter on my own as a child because two lesbians ran it and I think Mum thought they'd corrupt me or something. I used to go in all the time anyway and was very sad when May and Jenny retired. And quite recently a video rental shop opened. We feel very modern and upmarket having this within walking distance.

I tell Mum and Dad where we're going as we head out. It's only late afternoon but it's Sunday and most people are inside, sleeping off their Sunday roasts. The grey clouds from this morning are still above and they seem to be getting heavier. It's the only shop open, it is Sunday after all and we head inside. It's quite dark, having been an old DIY store and the racks of videos don't help.

We take out Batman Returns and grab a few bags of ten pence mix-ups before heading back to my house. We walk down the entry and suddenly Christian grabs my hand and pulls me into his arms just before we head into the garden.

The video clatters to the ground as we lock lips, arms and legs. It's quite dark down the entry when the gates are shut, and we both feel secluded and safe. He undoes the button and zip on my jeans and puts his hand down there and does strange but wonderful things with his fingers and I can feel myself pushing against him. I've no idea what he's doing but it feels so good and then like something bursts I feel like I'm floating.

My breathing is so fast that it takes me a few minutes to calm down, all the while he kisses me softly on my neck. I'm so stunned by what has just happened that I can't look at him and I just stand there, cradled in his shoulder.

'I didn't know it could be like that.' I say, when I've finally composed myself.

'Don't you worry, my love.' He kisses me on the nose. 'That's just the beginning.'

Chapter 23

It's Sunday evening and another week of work looms ahead.
We've been experiencing a heatwave here in the UK. Not
quite the stupid temperatures of last month where we tipped
forty degrees but we've been in the low thirties for a week
now and it is really starting to get people down. It just adds
to the general feeling of shiness that the whole country is
experiencing. Costs of everything spiralling further and
further out of control. Poor old Martin Lewis the money
expert doing all he can to help but forewarning of even
higher energy bills and now, to "help" manage our money
better they're going to increase the price cap every three
months rather than six. Can someone tell me how that's
actually going to help? Surely it just means we pay higher
bills more often. Why can't they just stop putting the price
up? Normal people simply can't afford it and we're basically
going to work just to live. No spare money for little luxuries
and the possibility of a holiday anytime soon is non-existent.

I've got the windows open and the fan on but still there's no
breeze in the house. It's eight thirty and Alexa is telling me
that its twenty-eight degrees. Twenty-eight degrees at this
time of night is almost unheard of in this country. I'm just
starting to get better sleep now my HRT has kicked in but
with the weather as it is, sleep is virtually impossible and to
add to my woes, my ankles and feet have decided to swell
up. Being a woman over forty is not all it's cracked up to be.

Antiques Roadshow is on, but I'm not really watching it. I'm scrolling through social media instead. I've got myself on Twitter and started following some fellow writers and started getting a vague idea how to get published. It is an absolute minefield if I'm honest with you and I haven't written any since I sent it to Joey, and he's been noticeably absent. Therefore, I am assuming what I wrote is shit. I know it's only one person's opinion and a person who up until a few weeks ago I hadn't spoken to for over thirty years but still.

The afternoon was spent with my daughter catching up on the latest episode of Teen Mum UK and I was suddenly struck by how little time I had left with her living in this house. She's twenty-two now, planning to move out and live with her boyfriend soon and I find I'm a mixture of happiness and downright utter wretchedness.

You bring these babies into the world and hope that they grow up to be well rounded adults and of course you want to see them find love with a partner who will respect them and treat them in the way that they deserve. However, when that happens, all you want to do is hold them tight against you and keep them safe at home. I can remember people telling me it would flash by in the blink of an eye, I never believed them but by God they were right.

It doesn't feel like five minutes since I was pushing her on the swings at the park after walking back from school. Now here she is, all grown up, able to drive and right at the start of her adult life. I guess that's how my parents must have felt too, although me moving out was a really quick decision, it wasn't planned, it just sort of happened.

'Mum!' Daughter calls from upstairs. 'I can't find my uniform.' She's currently on her final placement for university and all signs are that the place she's at will offer her a permanent job there.

'It's in the airing cupboard.' I call back, *where it always is.* I mutter under my breath but at least she's getting things ready now and not doing her usual trick of rushing round five minutes before she should be leaving.

'No it isn't!' I heave myself off the sofa and walk up the stairs one at a time. My ankles and knees cause me so much pain now that I have to take them this way. I know full well that when I get there, her uniform will be exactly where I said. But like everyone else in the house, if it's not holding up a little flag saying 'here I am' then it's not there. Of course, it is there. It's hidden underneath a few shirts and a pair of jeans but it's there all the same. 'Thanks Mum.' She disappears into her room and I have a wee while I'm upstairs. Always have a wee when you can, you never know what might happen.

Like when the bathroom door decided to lock itself from the inside. It was an absolute nightmare; we had to borrow a neighbour's ladder and climb in the window to open it. Luckily the window was open or I don't know what we'd have done. And Claire who now lives in London, makes it an absolute priority to always go for a wee before getting on the Tube because you never know when one might break down and over forty-year-old bladders are not the most reliable.

It will be quiet when she's gone that's for sure.

There's a chat notification on my phone when I get back downstairs. It's from Joey.

I love it. He says simply. *It's so real and totally from the heart and the way you end each chapter, I just want to keep reading and reading.*

You're not just saying that are you? This is my first fear and why I didn't share it with my best friends. *I want you to be completely honest with me.*

I am. He continues. *It's so genuine and honest and I hope you don't mind but I've sent it to a friend of mine who works in publishing. Just a small indie press and she said she'd give it a look over.*

I'm not quite sure how I feel about this. It will have goodness knows how many grammatical errors, missing punctuation and stupid spelling mistakes. I always considered myself proficient at English, but I wouldn't have a clue when and where to use a semi colon and if I've got too many adverbs, I'm just writing it because it needs to come out.

It's really helping me cope with everything that's going on with Mum. I'm not sure how it does it, but it does. Maybe it's just that I'm not thinking about things and keeping my mind occupied with something else. She's had her bloods done and on Wednesday is the start of her two-week isolation so we're all keeping away as we can't risk her catching Covid and then not being able to have the operation. Honestly, I don't think she'd cope with any more waiting.

Her one-hour naps have turned into three-hour naps and she's setting her alarm to make sure she gets up and walks around a bit because she's worried about blood clots. As if she hasn't got enough things to worry about right now. She does say her appetite has improved a little so at least there's something positive.

Have I done something I shouldn't have?

I'd forgotten I was talking with Joey.

No, it's fine. It is fine isn't it? I'm not sure. What if she doesn't like it? What if she says it's rubbish? But then, and I think I'm more scared of this, what if she says it's good?

What happens then?

Her opinion is only a subjective one anyway. Just get it finished and then go from there.

I've lost a little of the enthusiasm for it now. Maybe I shouldn't have shared it with Joey, but then I didn't know he was going to send it on.

I wish him goodnight and tell the kids I've got a headache and I'm going to bed early. I tell Alexa to play the Bridgerton soundtrack while I drift off to sleep. I was planning to read but I don't think I can concentrate. I'm not normally a fan of classical music but I love the way they've made modern songs sound like they're from the 19th century. Like when they walk into a ballroom and Ariana Grande is playing, pure genius. I absolutely adore the series, can't wait for season three and I'm not even the slightest bit in love with Jonathan Bailey, no Sir, not me.

Waking up the next morning, surprisingly refreshed. I felt a sudden urge to get back to the story and picked up my laptop whilst eating toast and drinking tea. I think the dream I had about Jonathan Bailey and Rege Jēan Page might have had something to do with it. And although I hadn't intended the novel to be a romance, I'm finding that it is. My own experiences and those of my friends when pieced together make a brilliant story and I'm enjoying the will they won't they bits so much.

I'm certainly no expert in writing but I've read enough books and seen enough films to know what I like and enjoy about romantic stories. The build up to a relationship, an almost kiss, sometimes they can be just as passionate as the sex. Lingering looks across a room, being within touching distance but not actually being able to touch. No wonder there were all these heaving bosoms in corsets in the past. Could you imagine being totally in love with someone, and not even being allowed to be alone with them until you are married when all you want to do is rip their clothes off? Surely basic human nature hasn't changed over the years and our ancestors must have been just as interested in sex as we are, probably more, especially the ladies. How frustrating.

Daughter calls goodbye before heading off and I realise that I am going to be late for work, again. It's a good job I can work flexible hours and just stay over. I'm loathed to leave my story but unfortunately that isn't what pays the bills. There's no time for a shower so a spritz of dry shampoo and an overdose of perfume will have to do. I pretty much work on my own so if I do smell it's highly unlikely to offend anyone.

I plug my phone into my aux socket and allow the playlist to shuffle. I find it always seems to know what I want or need in any given situation. I song I haven't heard in ages comes on and once again I'm back with Christian.

Chapter 24

Monday morning arrives like a shock and I'm still floating from last night. What Christian did was just mind blowing. I've experienced nothing like it before. It felt so wrong, but so deliciously right all at the same time. I haven't been able to look my parents in the eye since and was glad that we just spent the rest of the night in my room. Surprisingly, we actually watched the film. Michelle Pfeiffer looks incredibly sexy as Cat Woman and I just loved the song by Siouxsie and the Banshees called Face to Face.

After what happened in the entry, I thought we'd do more, but whether Christian didn't want to or was waiting for me to make a move, I don't know. I still find it hard to bring these things into conversation.

I stretch out in my bed, smiling for what must be the thousandth time at the memory, and I can't help my mind wandering off into the future and what sex with him will be like. There is of course no doubt in my mind at all that we will have sex, and soon if we can find somewhere to be alone.

Just think, a week ago today was when I first saw him and in one breath it feels like a moment but in another it feels like forever, as if he's always been part of my life and I didn't know a time when he wasn't in it. Do I love him? That's a tough question after a week, and what exactly is love?

There are so many types of love, parental love, sibling love, friends and then this romantic one, where you want to press your jiggly bits together and shove your tongue down each other's throat. Surely that's just lust, though. Love, like my parents and grandparents, is built over years. That reliance on each other, the trust and friendship that can only come from sharing so many experiences over time.

The threatened rain from yesterday has arrived, so I dress appropriately in a comfy sweater and jeans, black boots and grab my coat before heading downstairs.

'Breakfast young lady.' Mum scolds me from the kitchen. 'I don't care if you're running late.' She stops me before I can protest. 'You always make time for breakfast, even if it's just a banana or something.' I take a banana and an apple to please her and shove them in my bag. I'm not hungry in the slightest. This thing with Christian gives me permanent butterflies and I feel sick, but it's a nice feeling, not like the one when you're actually ill.

'See you later.' I pull up my hood and take a deep breath before plucking up the courage to go outside in what has now become a torrential downpour. The weather is funny like that in the UK. We swing from one extreme to the other.

I resist the urge to run. I'll be soaked by the time I get to school either way. A horn beeping behind me makes me turn around and there, like a knight in shining armour, well a shining car, is Christian.

'Need a lift?' He shouts through the tiny gap in his window. I don't bother to answer and rush round to the passenger side where he has unlocked the door from the inside and pushed it open, so I don't need to be outside any longer than I have to be. 'You're all wet.' He says and I blush instantly at the innuendo.

He realises what he's said and his face does that incredibly sexy thing he does where he sort of bites his bottom lip and raises his eyebrow. God! I just want to jump on him when he does that. Will it always be like this? These urges. Surely not. How does anyone ever get anything done with these feelings running through their body all the time?

'We're already late, you know.' I can't believe what I'm suggesting, or that I'm even thinking about it. I've never skipped class in my entire life, not once. I've never played hooky, ok, I may have pretended to be sick a couple of times whenever we had to speak in front of the class at school. I hate doing things like that. It was bad enough when Mrs Pickerell used to make us stand up and walk round the room doing times tables in maths in fourth year junior school.

We all had to stand up, and she made us answer in turn. If it was a tricky one like eight, you'd try and work out what your question was going to be but then you'd get caught out if one person got it wrong. That threw the whole thinking ahead system out.

'I'd best put my foot down then. Can't have you getting another detention with Mrs Bacon and me not being there to protect you.' He laughs and shifts into first, completely misunderstanding my meaning.

'I mean, we're already late.' I'm obviously not very good at this flirting thing.

'I know, I know.' He heads through Middle Avenue so he can go round the block and be facing the right way to get to the crossroads. 'I never knew you were so eager to get to school.'

I roll my eyes, but he can't see me. 'I'm saying we're already late.'

'I heard you the first time.' I can tell he's getting annoyed.

'Jesus Christ Christian.' I don't mean to yell, but I'm getting exasperated. 'We're already late so how about we skip first period altogether and you know, go somewhere?' I surely don't have to spell it out any clearer than that.

'Oh.' I know now that he finally gets it and when we get to the crossroads, he turns left rather than right for school and I don't know if I'm feeling daring about skipping school for the first time ever or for being suggestive.

The Milk Bar doesn't open in rainy weather, there's no point, no customers, so the car park is empty when we pull up. Christian turns off the engine and we both unclip our seat belts and just stare at the rain lashing down on the windscreen. It's that heavy now, it's practically a river running down the glass and you can hear it thudding on the roof.

We just sit there, the pair of us, staring at it. Neither speaking, not touching, just sitting. It's like we know exactly want we want to do but if we do, there's absolutely no coming back from it. Our relationship will have moved to a different level entirely and although my body is screaming out for it, my head isn't sure it's ready yet. It doesn't mean I can't kiss him, though.

And kiss him I do.

He moves at the exact same time I do and now we are facing each other. I wonder if he was about to do the same thing, or he just saw me out of the corner of his eye. He's looking at me, one hand running through his hair, and I've learnt quickly that this means he's nervous or unsure. I'm nervous too.

After what happened last night, now, being face to face with him in such close proximity, I'm embarrassed. He's had his hand on my most intimate parts. He's made me feel things I've never felt before, things I'd only ever read about or seen in films. Well, I didn't exactly see more implied.

Then he bites his lip and looks up at me through downcast eyes. A primal instinct takes over and I kind of lunge at him, grabbing his shirt by the collar and kissing him so hard I think I might have hurt him. I needn't worry; he matches my passion kiss for kiss, caress for caress.

Before either of us has even paused for breath, we are naked above the waist, shirts and jumpers thrown onto the back seat, hands exploring each other like we've never touched skin before. He kisses me in the hollow where my neck meets my clavicle and I arch against him, moaning a little and weaving my hands into his hair.

It might look romantic in the movies but making out in the front seat of a smallish car isn't the most comfortable, especially as both of us are quite tall and there's a handbrake in the way.

'Shall we move into the back?' He suggests and I nod, but this is easier said than done. His car is quite low. We're tall and trying to clamber through a six-inch gap and over the front seats proves near impossible until Christian reclines his seat, clambers onto the back and pushes it back up. I do exactly the same and now we are sitting, face to face again, half naked on his back seat with the rain streaming down outside.

I feel on show and suddenly shy and I cross my hands over my boobs. He shakes his head at me and gently lifts my hands away, replacing them with his own. He doesn't do anything but rest them there, waiting to make sure that I am ready before slowly caressing them. His eyes are on my chest the whole time, and this just makes it more sensual. I lean back against the side of the car, it's a two door, so there are no handles in my back, but I can feel the cold of the glass and it's soothing on my hot skin.

His eyes flick to mine as if seeking consent and I nod, knowing exactly what he is asking for as he captures my mouth for a kiss before moving slowly down to my breasts. He takes each one in turn, doing wonderful things with his tongue, and I feel like I might explode with the ecstasy of it all.

'Touch me.' He asks, and I tentatively place my hand on his jeans. 'Really touch me.' His voice is almost unrecognisable, so deep and quiet in its tone, and I reach inside his jeans. He feels soft and smooth and hot and throbbing all at the same time. 'Oh God Charlie.' I sense the desperation in his voice and it gives me confidence. I've no idea what I'm doing, but it feels right as I move my hand up and down the length of him. There isn't much room in his jeans, and he breaks away for the briefest of moments to undo his fly.

A loud banging on the roof of the car makes us stop guiltily. We hurriedly grab our clothes and look at each other. The banging comes again.

'What is it?' I got my jumper on and Christian has his shirt back on but is struggling to do it up. The back of his car has tinted windows and with the rain we know no one can see in but we can't see out either.

'Fucking hell!' The F word is a rarity. I've never used it in my life and it sounds odd on Christian's lips.

'Jesus Christ!' I see now what he's looking at. There's a blurry figure looking through the driver's window. 'Who is it?' I ask, knowing full well he has no more idea than I do.

The banging comes again and Christian reaches forward and opens the window a little.

'You haven't seen a little white dog, have you?' A male voice asks. 'I've been looking for her for over an hour, think the rain has spooked her.'

'No, sorry.' Christian says.

'Ok, sorry to disturb.' And the man disappears again.

We both flop back on the seat in total desperation.

'It's all a bit hopeless, isn't it?' I say and he nods in agreement before we clamber back into the front seats and head to school.

Chapter 25

I flick through the diary and the rest of September, all of October and the first half of November are blank. I didn't feel like writing at the time, but I can remember it all so vividly. This was when Grandad was diagnosed with a brain tumour and died exactly six weeks after he first fell ill. He stayed at home and fought all the way to the end, but it was heart-breaking to watch this strong, healthy man fade to nothing. It was my first experience of human death and the first time I ever saw a dead body.

My cousin and I had said goodbye to him just an hour before. His breathing was so slow and each breath got further and further apart. I remember Mum telling me a few years later how she and her sister would look at each other and then at him, praying he was finally at peace and out of pain yet praying for him to take just one more breath, for him to still be alive. Then he would gasp, and the cycle would begin again.

Eventually though, the gasp never came, and we were ushered in again to say goodbye once more. His body was still warm, and his face still slightly pink. I kissed him on his cheek, told him I loved him, and burst into tears. I visited him again at the chapel of rest and I wish that I hadn't, I wish that I'd left my last memory of him as this. Like the last memory I have of my other grandad is of him waving goodbye from the window. I didn't know he'd die that night. I'd have hugged him so tight if I'd known.

The chapel of rest was cold, like a freezer, and Grandad was dressed in a shroud instead of clothes. I still don't know if this was because he was Catholic or because that's what Nan wanted. But he looked so unlike my grandad. His hair wasn't right and one of his eyes was slightly open. He was grey and cold, felt and looked like marble. I couldn't get out of there quick enough.

He was buried a week later and I can remember laughing with my cousins in the funeral car as we followed the lead car and the hearse. I felt so very guilty for laughing when he was lying dead in the coffin in front of us. I told Nan, and she said Grandad wouldn't have minded and would have been laughing along with us. That cheered me a little.

I saw Christian, of course, but it was nothing like that first week. He knew exactly what I needed and just used to hold me as I cried or talk with me if that's what I wanted. He also sat in silence if I wasn't in a chatty mood. I failed my driving test again and missed his eighteenth birthday but promised to celebrate it at some point.

It doesn't feel like that now though. It doesn't feel as bleak and helpless as it did back then. Of course, treatments have moved on and Grandad's was terminal from the first diagnosis or perhaps it was being a teenager and now I'm an adult trying to keep everyone else's spirits up and not wallow in despair myself.

Work was its usual hive of activity, emails, holiday requests, overtime hours to check. Sometimes I get frustrated with the humdrum. The same old, same old, over and over again. Same old rubbish, just a different day. I've prepared for the end of the month, making sure everything is as ready as it can be in case I can't get into the office. I've booked the Friday off; we're closed for the bank holiday and then it's Mum's operation on the Wednesday. I'm kind of doing a mini isolation to keep her as risk-free as possible when I drive her to the hospital.

I've said I'll pick her up and take her in. Rob is doing the Covid swab on the Sunday. It makes more sense for me to do it. I work near the hospital and have a parking pass so I can just drop her off, go to work and then pop by afterwards and take her things to her. I doubt she'll be up for visitors that night. I remember my post appendix removal. I don't think I came round properly until the next day. I remember blurred visions of nurses checking my obs and asking me things, with mumbled replies, but that's about it.

'Why won't you have your things with you?' I asked as we chatted about what she'd need and want.

'It says in my letter that I might not have a bed before I go down and what if I'm not on the same ward and I have to go to intensive care or something like that?' Ever the optimist my mum.

'Then your bag stays with you.' I'm sure I remember travelling around the hospital with my overnight bag on the bed. 'Or the porters move it for you.'

'But what if someone steals it?'

'Why would someone want to steal your granny nighties, wash bag and puzzle book?' I'm trying to lighten the mood, but she wasn't having any of it.

'You hear all sorts of things about hospitals.' She then tells a tale of so and so whose best friend's neighbour's uncle's sister-in-law had her phone stolen while she was having a hysterectomy.

'I've never heard anything of the sort, Mum, but if it makes you feel better, I'll keep your stuff with me and bring it in after, once you're feeling a bit more with it.' I'm not sure what she'll do when she wants a shower or goes to the loo, probably take her whole bag with her into the bathroom.

I do love my mum and her little foibles. Of course, they can be so infuriating sometimes, but they are part and parcel of her and we wouldn't have her any other way. It wasn't always like that of course. She wound me up something chronic as a teenager, but as you get older and have children of your own, you realise that she was only doing her best.

Children don't come with a manual. You don't have a baby and instantly know how to look after them. You just sort of learn as you go along, listen to advice from friends and family, but ultimately you do what's right for you and your baby.

Take breast feeding. It's drummed into you over and over again, 'breast is best' and I'm sure all the research shows it is, it's natural but it's far from easy and what if you can't do it, you can be made to feel a failure.

I leaked from week twenty of my first pregnancy, had no milk after my daughter was born and she was on formula by two weeks. Couldn't fill my son up and when you're sitting in bed at two in the morning after being awake for an hour, sore nipples, and all you want to do is stop him crying and both of you get some sleep, then onto formula. Both my babies have grown up into perfect human beings. If you can breastfeed, that's great. It makes it so easy those first few days, no sterilising etc…but if you can't or don't want to then don't. Simple. Like most things in life and this takes a long time to learn, no one has the right to tell you what's best for you.

It doesn't stop me giving random bits of advice to my children, though, and receiving rolled eyes in response. I can't help it. It's not that I don't trust them or think they're stupid, but I've noticed in this generation a lack of common sense. Perhaps it was growing up in the 80s where health and safety meant standing in the gutter as the car went past, then going back to playing in the road that gave us Gen Xer's a better grounding. Maybe it was the lack of social media, growing up with grandparents that had fought one of the hardest battles ever, I don't know really, but we just seemed to have a natural understanding of things from a much earlier age than the youth of today.

Another random text from Mum asking me to order something from Amazon. Wipes?

'What do you need wipes for?' I ask, not having looked at it properly. Surely she can buy wipes on her online shopping.

'From what I've heard about the showers in the hospital, I won't be having one.' What's she been looking at? Trip Advisor for fucking hospitals?

'Of course you will.' I reply, thinking she's being a bit over the top. 'You just put your flip flops on, stand under the water and off you go.' It's not like you're sharing bath water or anything like that.

'No. I'll just take the wipes in.' If she could see me she would have seen me slap my hand to my forehead in total facepalm emoji. The wipes are biodegradable hygiene wipes. I just order them; tell her they'll arrive the next day and leave it at that. She'll do whatever she wants anyway, so there's no point wasting my breath on her.

Scrolling through Twitter, I see another celebrity has died, lovely Olivia Newton-John last week and now Darius Danesh. This one hits a little harder though. He was only forty-one and was found dead, alone in his US apartment. I was only playing his CDs in the car the other day. Yes, I still play CDs. I loved his voice, and he was so sexy, just my type, tall, dark and handsome with a deep sultry voice.

There's no reason given for his death as yet, just that there was nothing suspicious and it makes me realise how short life is. He was five years younger than me, that's all, barely halfway through and taken in a heartbeat. Things like this make you question your own mortality and I shiver. Time to make something of my life. By that I don't mean getting famous or rich but following my dream of being a published author or at least giving it a bloody good try.

I put my phone on charge out of the room. I find it so distracting next to me and I also scare myself at how 'itchy' I get when it's not near me. FOMO is real, and I don't really understand why. It's not like I've got a social media following hanging on my every Tweet and Facebook is mostly friends who I chat with in real life anyway.

I ask Alexa to shuffle songs by Darius and she puts Rushes on first. It's the perfect song for the chapter I'm heading into in my story. One where I'm drawing on my own experiences and I still blush now when I think about it.

Chapter 26

It's just over four weeks till Christmas, and suddenly the season is everywhere. The shops are decorated with lights, the Toys R Us advert is on the TV constantly and everyone is taking bets as to who will be the first house in the street to put their tree up. It's usually twenty-four at the top. We're never allowed to put ours up until exactly two weeks before.

Mum will send Dad up the rickety ladder to fetch the artificial Christmas tree, lights, and decorations down from the loft before we all help put them up. The familiar smell of the loft is synonymous with Christmas for me. Glass baubles that Mum and Dad have had since they were married in 1967 mix with modern plastic ones. Then the room decorations, which are meticulously put away each year in appropriately marked bags. Above the living room window or the wall adjacent to kitchen. Woe betide anyone who put them away in the wrong bag the previous year.

Christian and I are back to normal, stealing moments of passion, fearing getting caught at his house or mine. But I had an idea. A plan has formulated in my mind and as long as I can sneak certain things out of the house, then it will work.

He's asked me to meet him at our spot after school. I've already told Mum I'm staying late and technically; it isn't a lie. We've been hanging out there a lot lately, the little shed, but it's so cold now, we won't be able to do it for much longer. It never used to bother me, I wore a hat and fingerless gloves to read and I'd sneak a blanket in so it was ok, in fact, because it was sheltered it was slightly warmer than being outside eating lunch.

He had a free afternoon, but I had double history and Mrs Bacon carried on talking after the bell, so it's now almost half three. There are a few lads on the football pitch and Mrs Royston has the school hockey team practising. I really don't miss PE, especially in the winter. Tiny little black skirts over shorts and hockey sticks on cold shins. I shiver just at the thought.

There's no one in this part of the field, so I sneak through the gap and then into the shed and the sight before me makes my heart jump for joy.

On the floor, Christian has laid a thick duvet and then scattered cushions on top. There are two glasses and a bottle of Lambrusco and he's put candles around the place. It feels so warm and inviting.

'I didn't think you were coming.' He says, standing up to take my hand as I walk in. He closes the door behind me before leading me onto the floor to sit down.

'Bloody Bacon, she wouldn't shut up.' I look around and notice he's filled in all the gaps in the walls to stop drafts and has even hung some thick curtains at the window. 'You've been busy.'

'I've had a whole afternoon.' We're sitting opposite each other. 'But I've been planning it for weeks.'

'And me.' I say. 'I was going to do something similar, but nowhere near the grand scale of this.' I hadn't even thought about curtains. 'You've got a draft excluder.' I notice the stuffed, knitted sausage dog that is now lying across the bottom of the door. It looks like something my aunt would make.

'I brought some things here last night. Honestly, school is so spooky in the dark with no one around.' He admits. 'Really put the willies up me. Every little noise I thought was a ghost.'

'It is greatly appreciated.' I kiss him. 'Honestly Christian, it's just lovely.'

'I just thought we needed a little space for ourselves.' He stares at the floor and starts messing with the laces on his trainers. Another of the things he does when he's anxious. 'For, you know.' He doesn't look at me and I can sense he's nervous. We've been together for over two months now and done nearly everything except have sex, but we still feel nervous about it. 'If you want to that is.' He looks up at me, his hair desperately needs cutting and his fringe falls into his face constantly.

'I want to.' I say simply. And I do, so very much. I'm ready now. I trust him whole heartedly and I'm pretty sure I love him, although I haven't actually said it. But do I want to have sex with him here, in a shed, on the school grounds, no matter how lovely he's made it. But if not here, then where? It was what I was planning to do. Maybe that's the problem, maybe we're thinking too much about it.

'But not here.' He says exactly what I'm thinking, and I shake my head. 'I don't want our first time to be here either.' I sigh in relief. 'Second time maybe.' He laughs and leans over to open the wine. His arm brushes against me and I feel that familiar frisson of excitement course through me at his touch.

'Do you think we're overthinking it?' I ask, taking a glass from him. 'It's like at the beginning, before Grandad died.' I swallow hard but manage to keep the tears at bay before continuing. 'We couldn't keep our hands off each other, could we?' He nods.

'We can't really keep our hands off each other now.' As if to emphasise the point, he kisses my neck. 'Let's face it, I could ravage you right here and now if it wasn't for Mr bloody Wright blowing his whistle every five minutes.'

'Bit of a buzz kill, isn't it?' I can feel myself getting excited because his kisses have travelled upwards and I know very soon that they will be on my mouth. 'And now, here we are, practically alone and we don't want to.' He stops kissing me. 'That's not the right words.' I put my glass down, take his out of his hands and straddle him.

I don't say anything. I just undo my coat and slip it off. The cold air hits me and I shiver a little, but I'm determined to go on. He's leaning on the wall so I'm slightly higher than him now and as I lower myself down, he gasps a little. My hair gets in the way as I move to kiss him and I sweep it away angrily.

He reaches his hands up to cup my face and brings me closer to his. Our lips are so close now and I can feel how much he wants me even through two pairs of jeans.

'Goal!' someone shouts from outside and we both fall onto the floor and start giggling.

'What on earth are we going to do?' He asks, lying on the duvet and looking up at the ceiling.

'Mum and Dad usually go out on Christmas Eve.' I say hopefully.

'Christmas Eve.' He rolls onto his side, leans on an elbow, and looks at me. 'I can't wait till then.' He lifts up my jumper and kisses my stomach. 'Why don't our parents ever go out?' He's unbuttoning my jeans now.

'I think it's the time of year.' I say, trying not to think about why he's hitching my jeans down. 'Mum and Dad go out most weekends in the summer.' Oh God! He's taken my pants down now. The blood is rushing round my body so fast that I don't even feel the cold. 'In fact, they were away for a whole we…eeeekkkkk!' He places a hand over my mouth to silence me as his tongue does the most amazing things. I can't help biting his fingers and digging my hands into his hair as I writhe beneath him. Almost as quickly as he started, I feel myself exploding under his touch and I cry out against his hand.

He looks up at me over my stomach, resting his chin on my pelvis and Dear God, he looks so sexy right now. His hair is dishevelled from my wrangling, his eyes are so dark, and he has a wicked smile on his face, like he knows the power he has over me.

'Was that good for you?' He asks as I pull my pants and jeans up.

'I didn't know you could do that?' I sound like a twat, I know I do, but I honestly didn't know it was a thing. I'd heard of oral sex before, but I didn't really understand what it was and how you did it. 'Can I do that to you?'

'Of course.' He winks and unbuttons his jeans, but a noise outside startles us and we quickly and quietly blow out the candles and lean up against the door.

'Found it.' A male voice calls, scarily close to the shed followed by more rustling noise and then silence.

'Maybe not here, though.' I say, and he agrees.

'Let's get home, shall we?' I nod and we pack everything away, putting things in our school bags or wrapped in the plastic ones that were already there. Just before we leave, I pull him towards me and kiss him.

'Soon.' I promise.

I'm not quite sure what I'm promising him, alone time, returning the favour or the promise that we'll have sex. I'm not even sure it's even sex anymore. I love him. Quite plain and simple and it shocks me a little at the intensity of my feelings. We don't go a day now without seeing each other or at least speaking to each other on the phone and he has become such a part of my life now that I can't imagine him not being in it. I'm not even thinking about next September when he'll be off to university.

He takes hold of my hands, lifts them to his lips and presses a kiss on the back of each one.

'I love you Charlotte Anne Dean.' He says, he has never called me Charlotte, and it makes what he just said so sincere that I struggle to hold back tears.

'I love you too.' I fling my arms round him and hug him so tightly that he has to prise me off him after a while, pretending to choke.

It's dark outside as we walk home. The moon and stars light our way as we walk, hand in hand, our breath swirling like dragon smoke. And for now, it's enough.

Chapter 27

'Safe journey.' Tony calls after us as he drops us off at the train station on Saturday morning. It's two weeks till Christmas and everyone is on countdown. I love Christmas. It's such a special time, everyone seems happy, wishing random strangers a Merry Christmas and receiving cards in the post from people you met once on holiday. My mum has a whole notebook full of people like that. She sends about a hundred cards each year and gets about the same back. It takes her hours, but she sits at the dining table and just writes them all in one go and then sticks the stamps on. It's my job to post them. I've always done it. Mum and I used to walk to the post office and pop them in the post box, along with my letter to Santa.

'Thanks Dad.' Christian and I wave and head into the station, check the train time and platform, then it's up the stairs, over the bridge and onto platform three.

We're off to look at a university for the day. I have no idea which one it is, I've lost track. All I know is that it's a three-hour train journey with two changes. We were going to drive, but the Capri decided it didn't like the cold so it's in the garage my dad works in being looked over. I'm trying to be a good girlfriend and enthusiastic, but each time we go to one, my heart just feels like lead.

'You can always go yourself; you know.' Claire said over lunch the other day. She's slightly more relaxed now that all her applications have gone in. 'I know you applied to some local ones but there's always clearing.'

Even with the thought of being near Christian, university just does not appeal to me and as much as I enjoy school, not the exams and stuff, I just want to get a job now. Still no clue on what to do though.

'There's one.' The train to Birmingham is busy, but we grab two seats and plonk ourselves down. It's a short journey to New Street before changing to the next one. Christian has all the details written down on a piece of paper in his pocket, as well as the return journey. We had to come down in the week and sort it all out with the ticket office, but they were really helpful.

A bus has been laid on to take potential students from the station to the campus and I'm amazed at the amount of people getting on it. Lone students, couples, groups, and of course, people with parents.

The day passes in a blur of talks, tours and walking. So much walking that my feet are throbbing by the time we get back to the station. We're a little late, but we get on the train with a few seconds to spare.

'That was lucky.' Christian says, pulling out a can of Coke from his rucksack and a packet of Walkers crisps. We share the little picnic as he tells me his thoughts on the university we've just been to. He compares it with the other ones and decides it would probably be his second choice. His current favourite is one in Yorkshire, close to where one of his aunts lives and she said he could stay with her in term time, which would help with the cost of everything.

Before I knew it the motion of the train and the soft lull of Christian's voice had sent me to sleep.

'Where are we?' I ask, waking up as the train jolts to a stop.

'I don't know.' Christian sounds panicked. 'I fell asleep.' He pulls out his piece of paper. 'Either we missed the stop or got on the wrong train.' We both look out of the window and can see we're at a small station with the name Gainsbrook.

'I've never heard of Gainsbrook.' I look at him. 'Should we get off?'

'All change here.' My question is answered by the ticket conductor.

'Excuse me Sir', Christian asks. 'We need to get to Coventry.'

'Coventry?' He says. 'You're miles away from Coventry. You need a train to Woodborough and then Birmingham for Coventry.'

'Can we get a train to Woodborough?' I ask, hopefully.

'Not tonight.' He crosses his arms over his chest. 'Nothing going to Woodborough till tomorrow now.'

'Oh shit!' Christian says, earning a reproachful look off the man. 'Sorry Sir.' He apologises instantly.

'We really need to get home.' I say to the man who thankfully takes pity on us and softens.

'There's nothing that will get you home tonight, but there's a payphone by the ticket office to call your parents and a lovely B&B just outside the station.' He smiles. 'Tell Mrs Briggs that Arnold sent you and she'll look after you.' He heads off down the train.

'Shit Christian.' We make our way off the train. 'My parents will kill me and then they'll kill you.' The cold hits us as we step onto the platform. 'What time is it?' I look up at the station clock. 'Bloody hell, it's nine o' clock.' Now I'm the one who's panicking. 'I need to ring Mum and Dad; we should have been home by now.'

'You ring yours and then I'll ring Dad.' Christian says, handing me ten pence. 'He was supposed to pick us up from the station at eight, so I hope he's gone back home. Otherwise I'll have to ring Mum to go and tell him and oh Jesus Christ.' He sweeps his hand through his hair. 'What a fucking mess.'

The phone call to my parents was worse than expected. I had threats off my dad coming to pick us up but then realising he couldn't because he'd had a few glasses of wine. Rob was out and Mum would never drive anywhere she didn't know. Tony was far easier and had actually forgotten he was picking us up in the first place but promised to come and get us the next day if we'd let him know what time.

'We'd best hope this Mrs Briggs has some space for us.' I take his hand and as we walk through the station and out into the frosty air, I realise something. We're alone. Actually alone. No threat of anyone interrupting us at any time. I shiver. Christian thinks I'm cold and lets go of my hand to wrap an arm around me.

'That must be it.' He points towards a detached house, with welcoming lights in the windows, festooned with fairy lights on the outside and a sign reading 'Mistletoe Inn'. Below, a sign reading, 'No Vacancies'. 'Shit.'

'Let's try anyway.' We walk up the path and knock on the door. Almost instantly a rather stern woman appears.

'Yes!' she snaps.

'Erm…we…were…erm…' I'm lost for words. She reminds me of Mrs Bacon and I lapse into full on naughty child mode. 'Wondering if…you er…had a room free?'

'Can't you read?' she exclaimed, pointing at the sign.

'Arnold sent us.' Christian steps forward.

'Well why didn't you say so in the first place?' Her whole demeanour changes as she opens the door wide and ushers us in. 'Come on my lovelies, you must be freezing.'

The house is delightfully warm, with a huge real Christmas tree in the large hallway. As soon as you walk past it, you can smell the fresh pine mixed with the wonderful smell of cinnamon that's coming from the kitchen.

'Thank you so much.' I say to who I assume is Mrs Briggs. I'm not quite sure what I'm thanking her for at the moment. We don't have a room, but at least we're not traipsing round the streets of Gainsbrook on a Saturday evening. I don't even know what the streets of Gainsbrook are like on any evening, but towns and cities always seem to be more chaotic on Saturdays.

'No need to thank me, my lovelies. Pop your coats on the hooks there.' I'm picking up a slight country accent, but as we have no idea what county we're in, I haven't a clue if it's a local one or not. 'I'm sure Arnold told you, but I'm Mrs Briggs and this here is my little bed and breakfast.' She ushers us into a room off the hallway. It's softly lit with yet another Christmas tree, slightly smaller than the one in the hall. 'Sit yourselves down there and I'll get you a nice glass of mulled wine.'

We sit down on the softest sofa imaginable and wait for Mrs Briggs to reappear.

'This is a turn-up for the books.' Christian says, stretching out his long legs and relaxing on the sofa. I'm not so at ease, however. I keep worrying about my parents and the rollicking I'll get tomorrow, but I also can't get the delicious thought out of my head that Christian and I are together, for a whole night. I sneak a peek at him, wondering whether he's thinking the same, but his eyes are closed, his head resting on the back of the sofa.

'Here we go then.' Mrs Briggs is back with two steaming mugs of mulled wine, hot turkey and stuffing batches and a plate of homemade mince pies. 'I wasn't sure if you'd eaten or not, so I just whipped you up a little something.'

'Thank you so much.' I feel I'm over doing the thankyous, but I was taught always to be polite, and she's gone to so much trouble already. 'We haven't eaten since lunch.'

We should have been home for tea and the packet of crisps we shared on the train all those hours ago had done nothing and we fall on the batches like beggars.

'I'll go and get your room ready. It's only a single I'm afraid so I'll put a camp bed in for the young man as well and get the fire going.' She winked at me. 'It's just up the stairs and to the left, number five.' She pops a key on the table. 'You've got your own ensuite, fresh towels and toiletries. No rush to be out in the morning.' She winks again. 'Just leave the plates here when you're done and head on up when you're ready.'

'Why does she keep winking?' I ask Christian when she leaves.

He chuckles softly. 'Why do you think?' And then he winks at me.

Chapter 28

I'm not sure if it's the wine or the situation, but I feel suddenly giddy and lightheaded as we walk up the stairs after demolishing the batches, two mince pies each and the wine. Christian shushes me as I trip and giggle on the top step and he takes my hand before leading me into the room.

'There's no camp bed.' I say, looking around. 'Mrs Briggs said she'd put a camp bed in for you.' I flop on the small single bed. 'Now where will you sleep?' The wine must have addled my brain.

'Of course there's no camp bed.' He takes off his shoes and then unties the laces on mine. 'There never was a camp bed.' I can't work out what he's trying to tell me. 'That's why she was winking. Just in case anyone else was around. I'm sure she's a respectable establishment and can't have people thinking she just lets young people turn up and share a bed.' Even in the nineties, it's still a little frowned upon.

'So where will you sleep?' I ask stupidly.

'With you.' He says softly, stripping me down to pants and bra and then gently getting me under the covers before taking off his own clothes, leaving just his boxers on and sliding in next to me.

He's lovely and warm and I snuggle my back against him, his arm across my chest.

'Night then.'

'Goodnight.' He says, kissing the back of my neck.

I'm cramped when I wake up and slightly disorientated, and it takes me a few moments to remember. As I stretch out, I can feel Christian asleep beside me, so I gently get out of the bed and go to the toilet quietly before grabbing a blanket against the chill. I then sit on the ottoman at the end of the bed, opposite the window. There's a small gap and a weak light is coming in, so I know it's morning. There's the sound of movement outside and the smell of bacon wafting through, and it makes my stomach gurgle.

Even with the tiny bit of sunlight, the room is still quite dark and terribly small, and I wonder if it's even a room Mrs Briggs usually rents out. There's a gas fire on low, giving off a reddish glow, and I turn back to the bed to look at Christian.

The covers are off him slightly and I can see his chest moving slowly up and down. One arm is under the pillow and the other is out to the side, as if he's reaching for me. I can't help myself, but I feel like crying and although I don't want to wake him, it turns into a full sob.

'Hey.' He's there in an instant, his arms around me. 'What's the matter?'

'I can't believe it.' I'm so annoyed and upset with myself. 'We had this whole room to ourselves all night, and we didn't have sex.'

'You were a little drunk.' He kisses the top of my head.

'So what?' I ask innocently.

'I'm not taking advantage of you when you're drunk.' He says matter of factly.

'But how is it taking advantage of me?' I ask again, placing my hand on his chest. 'We've been wanting to for weeks, months even.'

'Because at that particular time, Charlie, you were drunk.' He heads into the bathroom after I've stopped crying and comes back out a few minutes later. He looks glorious standing there, the light from the bathroom surrounding him. His hair is messy, of course, I dread to think what mine looks like, but it just makes him even more adorable. 'But you're not drunk now, are you?'

The look he gives me turns my insides to jelly and that feeling I'm starting to recognise as desire stirs in between my thighs.

'No, but…' He walks towards me slowly, like a lion hunting prey. It's only a few steps but it seems to take an age. 'Someone might hear us.'

'Who cares?' He's in front of me now and I back on to the bed. He kneels on the ottoman and then crawls on the bed after me, his hair flopping on either side.

'But I've got morning breath.' I can't move any further, the headboard is against my back.

'So have I.' He's almost on top of me now and I instinctively draw the blanket closer round me.

'But…' He rolls his eyes, collapses on the bed, and reaches over to grab his jeans. I feel like an idiot then because I think he's getting dressed but he pulls out a packet of Wrigley's and hands one to me, popping a strip in his own mouth. I do the same, mint tingling on my tongue. 'But…'

'No more buts.' He takes my hands that are holding the blanket together, and with no resistance from me, he moves it out of the way. Feeling shy, I attempt to cover myself but he shakes his head and moves his body in between my arms instead so that now he is almost on top of me, his hands resting on the headboard, either side of me and his hips are currently in between my legs. I can feel his excitement.

He kisses me, long and hard and deep, and I moan inside his mouth, feeling myself wriggling my hips against his. We've done nothing but kiss but the close proximity makes me want him so much.

'Have you got anything?' He knows exactly what I mean and reaches into his bag. I watch as he opens the packet, pulls down his boxers and carefully rolls the condom on his penis, squeezing the end. 'Why do you do that?' I ask, suddenly acutely aware of the size of it and where it's actually going to go.

'Gets rid of air bubbles.' He turns back towards me. 'Your turn.' He pulls down my pants, throwing them to the floor and I hitch down the bed, so I am totally underneath him now. 'It might hurt a bit.' I nod. 'There's nothing I can do to stop it, I'm really sorry.' He kisses me.

'I know.' It's probably the only thing I do know. Lyn and India had such different experiences with their first time and it's not something I feel comfortable talking about with my mum. 'Is it in yet?' I ask.

'Not yet.' He kisses me again. 'Are you sure?'

'I'm sure.' I nod and then feel him inside me. It's a weird sensation, like sticking your finger up your nose. But it doesn't hurt. Then I feel him thrust a little and I almost cry out with the pain of it but I bite my lip. 'I'm so sorry.' He kisses me.

It doesn't feel how I thought it would. In the movies it's all fireworks and gasping, but there's none of that. It felt so much nicer when he kissed me down there, but I can tell by the way Christian is moving that he's definitely enjoying it. Perhaps it's just men that get pleasure this way.

'Oh God!' He moans into my hair and becomes sort of rigid with a really deep thrust at the end, then collapses on me, kissing my face all over. 'Oh Charlie. I love you so much.' He kisses me before gently pulling out, then heads to the bathroom, he does look funny walking with a wrinkly condom on the end of his penis.

When he gets back into bed, he's still naked and pulls me close.

'Is it always like that?' I ask.

'It will get better.' He reaches down to touch me, but I push his hand away.

'It's a bit sore.' It feels like I'm bruised inside and I'm a little frightened to go and see if there's any blood.

'It will get better.' He repeats, pulling me even tighter against his chest and kissing the back of my neck. 'I promise.'

'Ok.' I say, not sure if I believe him or not, after all, up until five minutes ago he was a virgin too. Wow, I'm not a virgin anymore. I snuggle into his arms, content to just enjoy being with him.

I must have dozed off because the next thing I feel is Christian kissing my neck, waking me up. His hands are on my breasts from behind and I can feel how hard is he again already.

'I want you so much, Charlie.' He quickly slips another condom on and then I can feel him inside me, from behind. It doesn't hurt as much now and with him stroking my breasts at the same time, I can feel myself moving with him. 'I'm coming.' He whispers. 'I'm sorry, I'm coming.' And there's that final thrust again before he goes rigid and then relaxes. Is this how it's going to be?

But this time, he doesn't come out straight away and reaches a hand down, swirling his fingers around while he's still inside me and fondling one of my boobs.

'Oh Jesus, Christian.' I push myself against him, wanting it to stop for that glorious high but never wanting it to end and then that wave after wave of intensity as the pleasure washes over me.

'We are going to have so much fun.' He says after a second trip to the bathroom. 'But I think we should think about getting home.' That brings me back down to earth with a thump. Home. I don't want to go home.

'What's that noise?' Christian pulls on his shorts and jeans and heads over to the window and opens the curtains. 'Is it seagulls?'

'Charlie, you're not going to believe this!' I quickly pull my jumper over my head and jump off the bed. 'We're by the sea.'

This little bed-and-breakfast backs onto the most glorious sight I've ever seen. The sea is almost to the wall at the end of the garden and seagulls are squawking overhead, looking for food.

'How didn't we hear it last night?' I ask.

'Perhaps the tide was out.' He pulls me into his arms, and I feel so close to him, the closest I've ever felt to anyone. 'Are you hungry?'

'Starving.' He nods his head. 'Let's see if Mrs Briggs will feed us.'

A thought suddenly hit me. 'Have you got any money?' I ask, panicking.

'Yeah, why?'

'Enough to pay for this?' He nods and I relax instantly.

'I've got my cheque book as well.' He throws my pants and jeans at me. 'Now get dressed so we can eat.'

I head into the bathroom. There's a few spots of blood when I wipe but nothing worse than the beginning of a period. I wish I had a pad to put on but at least my pants are black. I wrap a few bits of tissue into my knickers and hold it in place as I pull them back up, just in case I start gushing with blood or something like that. Jodie at school told us her sister had to have a blood transfusion when she first had sex, but I think now that Jodie may have been lying.

Splashing water on my face, I try and smooth my hair a little, but it's not working, so the scrunchie round my wrist comes into play, yet again. I'm pretty much decided that I'm going to chop it all off at my next appointment. I look at myself in the mirror, wondering if I look any different, not that I can tell.

'Come on, Charlie.' Christian opens the door. 'I'm starving and I don't just mean for food.'

Chapter 29

We've missed breakfast, of course we have, but Mrs Briggs makes us a pot of tea and we help ourselves to cereal. I pour a bowl of muesli and then pick all the raisins out of it while Christian stares at me over his Sugar Puffs.

'What exactly are you doing?' He asks. 'Don't you like raisins?'

'I love raisins.' I search through the bowl and find a final one lurking, and deposit it on the side with the others. 'I just don't like different textures in the same mouthful.'

'You've lost me.' He shakes his head and I try to explain that I don't like soft things in crunchy food and vice versa. 'Is that why, when you have a roast, you eat each bit of food individually?'

I nod and pour milk into my muesli, satisfied that all the raisins have been removed. 'And always leave the meat till last, best part.'

'I love discovering new things about you.' He smiles at me over the table, and I get that feeling again because I know he isn't talking about raisins.

'Got everything you need, my lovelies?' Mrs Briggs asks after saying goodbye to her other guests. 'Now, I'm just saying this, and what you do with that information is entirely up to you two, but that room is free again tonight and I'm happy for you to have it for nothing, let's call it a two for one offer. Now, Arnold popped in this morning to tell me that the trains to Woodborough are at ten, two and four, Sunday service you see and whatever you do with that information is up to you as well.' And with that, she winked at me, then at Christian, and headed out.

'I love Mrs Briggs.' Christian finishes his Sugar Puffs and lifts the bowl up to slurp out the milk.

'Well, we've missed the ten o'clock train.' I look at my watch, sadness washing over me that we have to go home. 'We'd best get the two just in case there's any more trouble or disruption with the trains. I forgot about Sunday service. Shame, though, I'd like to have walked along the beach.'

'We can.' He pours another cup of tea from the pot. 'We just don't go home.'

'What? Ever?' I'm not sure why my mind even thinks this way. Probably because it was exactly what I was thinking at the time, Christian and I staying here forever.

'Don't be daft.' He laughs and almost spits out his tea. 'It would be lovely though, just you and me, by the sea.' He shakes his head. 'One day. But no, just staying another night. We could say there's a problem with the trains or something, no one would know.'

I shake my head firmly. 'I can't lie to my parents Christian; they'd never forgive me.'

'They'd never know.'

'I'd know.' And as much as I want to stay another night, I just can't do it.

As we head back up the stairs, Christian takes my hand. 'What if we didn't lie?' I look at him. 'What if we kind of stretched the truth?'

'I'm listening.' A little rebellious voice inside me says.

'What if we ring our parents after four and say we're really sorry, the last train has gone but we're safe and sound and being looked after in a local bed-and-breakfast?' He's looking at me so intently and I can see he's begging me to say yes.

'We don't have any spare clothes, toothpaste even.' My mouth already feels fuzzy and chewing gum just doesn't have the same effect.

'There's bound to be a corner shop around here somewhere.' I'm desperate to say yes.

'But what if my dad comes and picks us up?' I've had this thought running through my head since I spoke to Mum last night. Every time I heard a car door, I expected my parents to be standing outside.

'Did you tell them where we were?' I shake my head. 'And I didn't say either, so if we just don't say anything, it's ok.' He lifts his shoulders and opens out his hands.

'I'm not sure Christian.' He doesn't say another word and we carry on up the stairs, heading into our little room. I pull back the curtains fully and now the sun is shining on the sea and it is glistening. It looks so inviting outside, even though I know it will be freezing cold.

'Or I could just lock you in here and make love to you all day.' He comes up behind me and puts his arms around my waist, kissing my neck. I turn into his embrace and kiss him, weaving my hands up his back. 'That would just be wonderful, wouldn't it?'

I nod and let him lead me to the bed.

'You go first?' I push him towards the payphone in the station. We've spent the day walking along the beach, eating fish and chips out of the paper with wooden forks and generally just being together. Mrs Briggs was ecstatic when she heard we were staying another night and I've tried to ignore the sinking feeling in my stomach all day, but we can't put it off any longer.

'Get it over and done with.' He hands me the ten pence. 'My dad won't be bothered; he's probably forgotten I was meant to be at his this weekend anyway. It's only my car on the drive that usually reminds him and that's in your dad's garage.'

'Oh for God's sake.' I pick up the receiver, dial the number and push the money in as I hear a voice answer. It's Rob. I've never been so relieved to hear his voice in my entire life. 'Rob listen. Tell Mum and Dad, the last train has left, we're safe and sound, staying in a hotel (I use hotel because Mum can be a bit snobby) and we'll be home as soon as we can tomorrow.' I can hear Mum in the background, asking who it is and when Rob replies I can overhear her ordering him not to put the phone down. 'Money's running out, got to go.' And I hang up.

'See.' He kisses me. 'Wasn't that terrible, was it?' I shake my head.

'Only because Rob answered.' I laugh, feeling suddenly light and slightly naughty. I've never done anything like this in my life, always been a good girl, done as I was told, but this feels sort of wonderfully exciting. 'See you next weekend then, Dad.' Christian has already replaced the receiver. 'All done.' He rests his arm around my shoulders. 'Moonlight stroll?'

It's absolutely freezing and pitch black, but the town of Gainsbrook isn't very large and we've already found our way around most of it. We got some basic things from a small corner shop; I'd love a pair of pants to change into, but I bought some panty liners instead as the next best thing. Christian thought I'd come on; I don't think I'll ever forget the smile on his face when I said I hadn't.

There's something delightfully romantic about walking along the beach at night. I know it's not night exactly, but winter evenings are so long, it becomes night from around four.

'I'm never going to forget this you know.' Christian says to me as we sit on the back wall of Mistletoe Inn, staring out at the sea. 'It's like our first holiday.'

'Nor me.' I rest my head on his shoulder. 'It's been wonderful.' I want the evening and the night to last forever, but I know that it can't. Nothing lasts forever, and I shiver at this, remembering that come September he'll be away for weeks and weeks at a time.

'Let's go inside.' He kisses the end of my nose and I nod.

Mrs Briggs has left flasks of hot soup and fresh bread in our room and they're just what we needed to warm us up. I'm still shivering a little, though.

'Can you turn the fire up please?' I ask Christian and he reaches behind him.

'I know something that will warm you up.' He raises an eyebrow, takes my hand and leads me into the bathroom. The shower is hot and wet, like his kisses and we spend what feels like hours exploring each other, pleasuring each other. When we eventually get into bed that night, we take our time and when he's finally inside me, we come together and it's the most wonderful feeling ever.

'I love you Christian.' I feel like crying for some reason and I don't have a clue why. Perhaps it's all the emotions, the pent-up frustration of the past few weeks, or the fact that this wonderful little interlude has to end.

'Always, forever Charlie.'

Chapter 30

The drive to Mum's house takes me past the train station and although it's been improved lately, the entrance is still the same and I have flashbacks of Christian and I arriving back that Monday morning. Well, it was almost afternoon by the time we'd got out of bed and had breakfast and figured out the trains home. We found out later on that we were almost two hundred miles away from Coventry.

Mum was waiting at the station for us. She'd come on the bus as Dad and Rob were both at work and had taken the cars. Apparently, she had been there since nine. She made me feel about five years old as she dragged me onto the bus back home. Christian of course got the same one, but she totally ignored him, and he had to sit miles away from us.

We had the mother of all arguments that day and didn't speak civilly to each other for a week. She grounded me, of course, totally forgetting that Christian attended the same school and after three days she gave up. It took her a while to forgive Christian though, and he was met with icy stares for weeks. I also discovered that Rob had been a total ally and put the phone down as soon as Mum reached for it. She didn't speak to him all day, either.

'You got everything, Mum?' I ask from the doorway. It's early, half-past six in the morning. I'm trying to be cheerful on the outside, but inside I'm filled with dread.

'I think so.' She's at the door, looking the smallest and most scared I think I've ever seen her. Mums and dads aren't meant to be scared. They're the ones that are always brave and chase bad dreams away with a kiss and a cuddle. But not today. Today that's my job.

'Go get yourself in the car and I'll lock up and grab your bag.' I can't even give her a hug or a kiss in case of giving her bloody Covid. Even though I've practically self-isolated for a week and tested this morning, it's not worth the risk, so I just squeeze her arm gently as she walks past.

I lock the door, making sure that she is watching me doing it and check the handle three times before putting her bag in the boot. Nan is at the door as we reverse off the drive and I can see the worry in her face. She's buried her parents, a brother, a husband and a precious son-in-law. She's almost ninety-nine and has watched all her relatives and friends pass away and now, she's watching helplessly as her eldest daughter heads off to the hospital.

I know what she'll be thinking. I can't help thinking it too. I know Mum will be exactly the same, because no matter how skilled a surgeon, how routine an operation, there's always a risk.

We don't really talk on the journey; I don't think either of us is up to much small talk, so I've just put Cliff on my phone through the stereo and she seems content. The drive is uneventful, there's hardly anyone on the roads yet, it's still the school summer holiday, so half the usual traffic is missing. I grab a parking space easily then find a wheelchair for Mum. I know she wanted to walk in, but Rob said she struggled with her Covid swab the other day and it's a much greater distance to the ward.

'Can you grab my handbag please?' She gets in the wheelchair without protest, and I place her bag on her lap. It's only got a book and a couple of bits and bobs in. She'll be in a hospital gown for her operation and everything else is in the big bag ready for me to bring to her later on.

The hospital is already busy with staff and patients milling about, and I can smell toast as we go up the lift and off to the ward. I push the button on the door and a smiling nurse welcomes us, hands me a card with phone numbers on it and then takes Mum away. I wave at her through the door, mouth that I love her and then breakdown into tears as soon as she's gone.

When I'm back in the car, my phone pings with messages from friends and relatives and one from Joey. It makes me smile to know he's thinking of me.

I do my best to keep busy at work. After having time off, there's more than enough to do and Daz, the mechanic, keeps me supplied with cups of tea and dirty jokes. We listen to Radio 2's Pop Master as usual and I amaze myself by getting the three in ten, well it was Take That.

I'm trying my best not to keep checking my phone because when all is said and done, Mum doesn't have hers with her, so I've got absolutely no idea when she'll be out of theatre. I think she said she was going to ask a nurse to ring me and let me know, but I know how busy everyone gets.

By one, I'm getting a little twitchy and after treating myself to a McDonalds delivery, cheeseburger, haloumi fries and a raspberry ripple frappe (surprisingly I'm actually hungry), I open my phone and find a message from Joey asking to meet me for a drink in the hospital café.

Within seconds I'm out the door, shouting to Daz and in my car. Why the fuck does he want to see me? It can only mean one thing: something really bad has happened. I can't find a space, of course I can't, the hospital doesn't have anywhere near enough spaces, so I watch people coming back and following them, falling lucky when a lady realises my plight and tells me exactly the spot she's heading back to. I thank her profusely as she leaves and I slide my Astra straight in, surprising myself with the perfect parking first time out.

I wish now that I hadn't had that burger because it feels lodged in my throat and I want to throw it up, but instead I do my fastest walk run to the café and find Joey sitting at a table. He doesn't look overly worried, so I relax a little but then having not really seen him since I was fourteen, I have no idea what a worried Joey looks like.

'Do you want a drink?' I shake my head; I don't even think I could stomach water at this moment in time.

'What's happened? Is Mum ok?' He nods.

'I'm sorry, I should have realised you'd be worried.' He rubs a hand through his hair, still quite brown for his age, I notice. 'I just wanted to tell you in person. Are you sure you don't want a drink?' I can tell he's nervous and his nervousness is making me worse. I want to grab him and shake him. 'The operation went well.' I sigh. 'It's just a little bit more complicated than we thought.'

'Ok.' It's all I can think of to say.

'When we got inside, we could see that it had spread a little further than we first thought, so unfortunately it will be chemotherapy or radiotherapy in the very near future.' The whole of my body sags inside at his words and he places a hand over mine. 'It's still a good prognosis.' He smiles at me. 'She's back on the ward, very sleepy. We haven't told her yet obviously; we want you and your brother to be there, so we won't be telling her till tomorrow or even Friday.' I nod numbly, and then a beeping noise catches his attention. 'I've got to go.' He stands up and kisses me on the cheek. 'We'll get that tea another day, shall we?' And then he's gone, and I just sit there.

It takes me a few minutes to make a move and as soon as I'm outside with a signal; I phone Rob. He is, as predicted, quietly devastated. I fire off a message to the girls but no one else needs to know yet and I drive back to work where Daz makes me a cup of tea and then I just sit there, staring at the computer screen until the nurse rings to tell me I can see Mum.

Rob arrives almost at the same time, and we hug each other tightly before plastering on smiles and walking into the ward. Mum is groggy and tired, but the painkillers are doing their job and she manages to drink and eat a little. I lock her things away in the cupboard next to her bed and pop the key on a band around her wrist, something Rob remembered his wife doing a few years ago.

I drive home, still completely and utterly numb. I can't hide this from the kids, and we have a little sob together. I can't be bothered to cook, so I order them a pizza and have a long soak in the bath and then off to bed. By the time I wake up in the morning, they are both gone, their breakfast things in the sink and a little note from the pair of them saying 'love you xx'. I smile at the normality of the washing up and the thoughtfulness of the note.

A quick group chat with the girls before they head off to their various works and then I make a cup of tea, flick on the TV and prepare for a day of doing absolutely sod all. I want to wallow and be angry at the world, so I'm going to wallow and be angry at the world. There's a text from Mum saying she's been and had a shower, I knew she would, and that she's eaten toast and is now sitting in her chair waiting for the doctor.

I'm glad she's feeling positive and part of me wishes we didn't have to tell her, and I finally understand now why my nan didn't tell my grandad because she didn't want him to lose his spirit and his fight, but unfortunately, Mum has to know. It's not like sneaking a tablet into someone like we did with Dad, although that was a game in itself. He thought we were poisoning him and even the tiniest tablet would magically get stuck in his throat. No, there's no hiding this. She's going to be making regular trips to the hospital for the foreseeable future, and that's that.

Around twelve, I head upstairs and make the bed, tidy up a little and put some washing away. A car door makes me look out of the window and my heart lifts instantly at the sight. Before they've even made it to the door, I've opened it.

'I thought you might need a cup of tea.' In his hand is a cardboard carrier with two Starbucks cups in it. I'm so shocked to see him that I grab the carrier out of his hand, not caring if it spills, pull him inside by the collar of his shirt and slam the door behind him.

'I don't want tea.' I kiss him, hard, as if I'd never kissed anyone before. He matches me kiss for kiss and before we know it, he's stripped from the waist down, my nightdress is up around my neck and we're doing it on the stairs.

It is uncomfortable, painful and glorious all at the same time, and it's exactly what I needed to make me feel wanted and alive. I dig my nails into his back and wrap my legs around his waist, pulling him as close to me as I can. It's over almost as soon as it began and he collapses on top of me, breathing heavily.

'Well, I wasn't expecting that.' He says, kissing me gently and smoothing my hair out of the way. 'Shall we have that tea now?'

Chapter 31

The day I've been dreading has arrived and I groan as the alarm clock blares and I nudge Christian to turn it off. He reaches behind him and whacks it one, before putting his arm back around me and nuzzling my neck.

'Morning.' He whispers sleepily.

'Morning.' I repeat, kissing his arm before getting out of bed and into the shower.

He has a nice room at university, student halls, but found himself a job which has allowed him to pay for a private room with its own shower. He has to share a kitchen and living room still, but they seem a nice bunch from what I saw yesterday as me and his parents helped him to move in. They went home after dinner and I'm heading back home today because I start my new job in the morning.

I'm a trainee accountant at a local firm. Don't ask me why I chose accountancy. I like numbers and I've always been good at maths. My A Level results were, if I'm honest, totally shit, considering I only had two subjects. Claire got straight As, Christian ABBC and me, what did I get? Two Ds and a C in general studies. Who gets a C in general studies? Then I saw an advert in The Coventry Evening Telegraph advertising for trainee accountants to start in September and thought, hey, why not?

It took me five different interviews until I finally got offered a position. Of course it was the lowest paid one of the lot, £3449 per year, but they offered to pay my college fees and give me time off to study, so I shook Mr Luckman's hand gladly.

So, with those results, even if I'd wanted to, university was never going to be an option. I'm excited to start work, but leaving Christian is going to be one of the hardest things I'm ever going to do. We've spent virtually every day together and even managed nights together when our parents were away. We desperately wanted to go back to Mistletoe Inn over the summer, but Mrs Briggs was fully booked from May to September.

'Fancy some company?' I don't know why he asks; he comes in anyway and I'm not about to say no am I? He lathers my hair for me, it's still long and I wash his chest as he does mine and before I know it, we're making love, as we always do and God, I'm going to miss this. I went on the pill a few months back, just because I was getting so panicky each time my period was late, but we've become much more experimental without having to use a condom.

We even did it in the park over the summer, under a blanket, of course and hidden from view. We didn't go at it on the swings or anything like that and it felt exciting and dangerous and on the last day of school, after our final maths exam, we found ourselves back at the little shed and we did it there as well. We left it for some other invisible soul to find next term.

Christian has really helped me with all that. He's helped me realise that other people's opinions don't really matter in the grand scheme of things. If something is important to me, then the people who are important to me will realise that because as Dr Seuss said: Those who mind don't matter and those who matter don't mind.

He didn't end up going to any of his chosen universities in the end, because of his high results, he went through clearing and got into one he'd wanted to go to all along; it means he's even further away but he's happy and that's what counts the most.

We make toast in the shared kitchen, but I just pick at it and then all too soon, it's time for me to go to the station. I grab my bag from his room and when I return; I find him talking to a girl sitting at the very same table I was just sitting at. I've never felt a sensation like it before in my life, except maybe when Jenny bought her Sindy horse and carriage in for toy day once, but the feeling I have right now is like someone has taken a red-hot poker and shoved it straight through my heart and then pulled it out and shoved it in my stomach for good measure.

Please be ugly, please be ugly. I say to myself as Christian introduces me; he does use the term girlfriend, I'm pleased to hear.

'Hi, I'm Susie.' The girl turns round, and of course, she's one of the prettiest girls I've ever seen in my life. She's clearly wearing make-up, but it's subtle and enhances rather than masks. Her hair is so shiny it gleams, and her smile lights up her face. She stands up and she's shorter than me,

Ha!, but her boobs are huge, and her waist is tiny and when Christian stands up next to her she looks like she'd fit just under his arm. I shake the thought away and shake the hand she's offered me. 'Don't worry, I'll look after him.'

Oh but Susie, that's what I am worried about.

I'm trying not to be in a mood on the way to the station. I'm really not. I don't want our goodbye to be tainted in any way, so I give myself a stern talking to, plaster a smile on my face and put all thoughts of Sexy Susie out of my head and just enjoy mine and Christian's last few minutes together.

Before we know it, we're on the platform and the train has arrived. I kiss him so gently, so sadly, trying to pour all the emotion I'm feeling into this one kiss and then there is no more time, and the guard is calling all aboard and I have to go. The look in his eyes is heart breaking. He walks me right to the door and kisses me one more time before the guard comes along and closes it between us. The train moves off, and he holds my hand through the window as long as he can, running a few steps, but then the platform ends and his touch is lost to me.

I look back at him. He's mouthing something and tapping his back. I think he's saying bag, then he waves and is gone. I find my seat, pull out my Walkman and headphones and inside is a little red box, neatly tied with a bow. He must have snuck it in last night. I open it carefully. Inside is a cassette tape and in Christian's handwriting…Till I'm Home Again. I replace Now 27 with the tape and it's filled with our favourite songs, Pet Shop Boys, Kenny Thomas, Mariah

Carey and there's one on there that makes me cry, Love is All Around by Wet Wet Wet.

We saw Four Weddings and A Funeral at the cinema, and I absolutely fell in love with Hugh Grant and believe it or not, it was the first film we saw at the cinema together. The music gets me home and Rob meets me at the station with a brotherly hug and a 'cheer up kid'.

I wait by the phone all evening for Christian to ring, but he doesn't and when I try to ring the number he gave me it's permanently engaged.

'Everyone will be ringing their parents.' Mum says comfortingly and I'm sure she's telling me the truth and not just words to take my mind off things. I can't help feeling sad when I go to bed though.

It's the middle of the night when Dad comes into my room and shakes me awake.

'Phone call for you.' I look at him, dazed. 'It's Christian. Tell him not to make a habit of calling this late, but we'll allow it just this once.' He heads back to bed as I bound down the stairs.

'Hello?'

'Hi Charlie.' He's whispering. 'Did I wake you?'

'Of course you woke me, it's three in the morning.'

'I couldn't sleep. My bed is cold.'

'Mine too.' It feels so wonderful to speak to him.

'I couldn't get hold of the phone earlier. Every time I went to get it, someone else got there first or it was someone's parents ringing. Susie says it will calm down. She's repeating her first year, so she's showing me and the lads the ropes.'

I bet that's not all she's showing the lads.

The beeps start and I hear him fumbling for change.

'Quick, you need to put more money in.'

'Ah fucking hell.' And then he cuts off. Should I ring him back? I've no idea how much it costs at this time of the day. Is it still classed as the weekend or is it Monday morning now? I decide against it and as I can't ask Dad, I head back to bed.

I wish he hadn't mentioned Susie. I don't want to think about her or any of the other girls he'll come into contact with. India and Lyn came round earlier and told me that it basically boils down to whether I trust him or not. I do trust him with all my heart I said, it's girls I don't trust.

Look at Emma in sixth form, I said to them, she was determined to get Christian to go out with her, didn't give a shit about me.

'But she didn't get him, did she?' India reminded me.

'He's totally in love with you, don't you get it?' Lyn had piped in, but I'd shook my head.

'I'm fine when I'm with him.' It's true, I am. 'But away from him, I get all these doubts. He's so gorgeous, he could have anyone.'

'He's not all that you know.' I give Lyn a look. 'He's not my type at all.'

'We get what you see in him.' India had explained. 'But he's far too boy band for us. He's a lovely fella, though.'

Thinking back to their words makes me feel a little better and I somehow fall asleep ready for my first day at work. Then just as I'm about to leave, he rings to wish me luck and I drive to work, playing his tape and floating on air. Christian Sawyer loves me, and I love him, so no matter the distance, we'll be together.

Chapter 32

I hate Christian Sawyer, hate, hate, hate!

It's been over two months now since he left for his third year of university, and he hasn't been back once. I've a good mind to drive up there and have it out with him, but I haven't got a clue how to get there in the car, I always go on the train. Susie has sorted him and the lads out with new digs. They've been together the entire time and have all become firm friends. Susie has made her way round the entire group, and I'm not sure there hasn't been something between her and Christian. I went up in October for a long weekend and every time I came into the room, silence would fall as if there was some secret between them.

'Let's go to the cinema like old times.' India suggests. 'Claire's back from uni and we can grab something to eat after.' She flicks open the paper to check the listings. 'Long Kiss Goodnight with Geena Davis and Samuel L Jackson looks good. Let's face it, anything with Samuel L Jackson in is going to be good.' India has a tiny little crush on him, has done since Die Hard. There's us, all fawning over Bruce Willis and there's India crushing on Samuel L Jackson.

'I'm not really in the mood.' I just want to mope about, but she finally persuades me, well forces me after shouting to my mum that we're off to the cinema, phoning India and Lyn before we leave the house to tell them she'll pick them up on the way. We drive through the city, singing along to A-Ha and over to Walsgrave where The Showcase Cinema is, and I'm sorely tempted to head off to Tony's house.

'Four tickets for The Long Kiss Goodnight please.' India hands over the money and then we grab large tubs of popcorn and drinks. The film is an excellent choice, full of action and Geena Davis playing an assassin is pure genius, she's perfect for the role. 'You lot head to the car, I've just got to phone home, forgot to leave Mum a note.' She throws the keys to me, heads to the payphone outside, and the three of us walk to the car.

When she gets back, she's smiling and then Lyn and Claire start smiling too.

'Ok, what's going on?' I'm immediately suspicious. The last time the three of them looked like this was when Scott Griffin met me in Central Library after work experience and asked me out. The three of them had known for weeks.

'Nothing is going on, Charlie.' India puts the key in the lock but doesn't start the engine.

'Honestly Charlotte, you're so suspicious.' Lyn chirps from the back seat.

'Right, if you don't tell me what's going on, I'm getting out of the car.' I place a hand on the door, but none of them stop me.

'Go on then,' Claire urges. 'Off you go.'

'What?' I'm flabbergasted. 'You'd all leave me here.'

'You said you'd get out if we didn't tell you so out you get.' Lyn reaches from the back and pulls the handle.

'But…how will I get home?' I don't move. 'Stop being silly and let's just go and get something to eat.' We might be twenty-one and twenty years old, but sometimes we can still act like a bunch of kids.

'Nah, don't want to, now.' Claire sits back in the seat and folds her arms.

'Nor me.' Lyn follows suit.

'I think I might just sit here for a while.' India pulls down the sun visor and starts messing with her hair and then she adjusts her wing mirror. 'Right on time.'

I turn in the direction she's looking, and a familiar car pulls up behind and then alongside.

Hanging over the side, with his window down, even though it's one degree above freezing, is Christian. He smiles at me and despite how angry I am at him; I melt inside.

'Is someone in need of a lift?' The three of them burst into laughter and practically push me out of the car. Then India walks to her boot, pulls out my little travel suitcase and puts it in the boot of Christian's Capri.

'You'll be needing that.' She says, before jumping back in her car, Lyn clambering over into the front seat and the three of them waving and blowing kisses as they drive off.

'Where! The! Hell! Have! You! Been!' I punctuate each word with a whack of my bag after getting in the passenger seat.

'And it's lovely to see you, too.' He heads out of the car park and onto the M6. 'You cut your hair.'

'Don't change the subject.' I'm riled now. 'I'm so angry with you, hardly a word for weeks, no phone calls, no letters, nothing.'

'I've been busy.' He turns the radio on, but I turn it off straight away.

'I'm not done talking,' I shout.

'You're not talking though, you're yelling.' He's amazingly calm considering how irate I am. 'When you're ready to talk, I will quite happily converse with you on the subject of my absence. But in the meantime, I've got a long drive ahead of me and would prefer a little bit of music.' He turns the radio on again and this time I leave it on, folding my arms across my chest in an exaggerated manner.

'What do you mean by a long drive?' He knows he's caught my attention but refuses to speak and is annoyingly singing along to Oasis, Don't Look Back in Anger, purposely off key. 'Christian?' I ask softly.

'Yes, my love?' He turns his head very briefly to look at me.

'Where are we going? And why is my suitcase in the boot?' These are my most pressing questions.

'We are going somewhere, and your suitcase is in the boot because India put it there.' I look at him and can see a smile forming in the corners of his mouth. God, he's so bloody sexy, even when I'm angry at him.

'And where might that somewhere be?' I rephrase the question.

'Somewhere over the rainbow.'

'There isn't a rainbow.' I'm pretty sure I'm not going to get any answers out of him, so I just sit back in the seat and try and work out from the motorway signs where we might be heading. I don't have the foggiest and after two hours we pull into a service station to fill up with petrol. I'm still angry with him because he hasn't explained where he's been, but I'm totally intrigued now. I go to open the boot and put my handbag away, but he slams it down quickly.

'No peeking.' I fold my arms across my chest.

'It's a car boot.' I state. 'What is there to peek at?'

'You'd be surprised.' We get back in the car and head off on the motorway again.

'I take it my parents know where we're going?' Even at twenty and having been dating for three years, they still like to know where I am. Rob moved out in the summer to live with his girlfriend and the house hasn't seemed the same since.

'They know where we're going, but not why we're going.' Another cryptic clue. 'Only Susie knows that.' I bristle at the mention of her name, and he sees it. 'I honestly don't know what you have against her. She's been nothing but kind and friendly to me and to you.'

'I'm sure friendly isn't what she has in mind.' I turn to look out the window.

'For the millionth time, I have never had any interest in Susie or any other girl for that matter.' He places a hand on my thigh. 'It's only ever been you, Charlie, always, forever.'

'I'm sorry.' I turn to face him.

'Now, about the hair.' I reach a hand up to the very short, razored edge on my neck.

'Don't you like it?' I ask. It's something I did a few weeks ago, I really had got fed up with it being knotty all the time and just went to my hairdresser and had it chopped off. It feels so much lighter now and it dries on its own in half an hour instead of spending hours under the hair dryer.

'It doesn't matter whether I do or don't.' He smiles. 'It was just a bit of a shock.'

'Well, if I'd seen you, perhaps I would have told you.' I tease.

'Touché.' He remains silent for a while and I think he's concentrating on the road. 'Just have a look in the glove box, will you. Dad wrote me out some instructions and I can't remember which junction we get off at.'

I pull out the map of the British Isles and find the piece of paper. Unfortunately, there are no place names, just roads and junctions.

'It says junction five.' I read. 'Then four miles and take junction thirty-three and then it says it should be signposted from the roundabout.'

'Brilliant, next junction then.' He gets into the left-hand lane, skilfully manoeuvring between a lorry and a car towing a caravan. It's then that I see a familiar name.

'Are we going to…?' I don't need to finish my sentence and Christian just nods and I squeal in delight. 'But why all the secrecy?'

'Just wanted it to be a surprise, that's all.'

'Well, it's certainly been that.' About fifteen minutes later, we are pulling into the welcoming sight of Mistletoe Inn and Mrs Briggs runs out to greet us.

'Oh my lovelies, it's so good to see you.' It's dark again, like the last time we arrived and being close to Christmas the house is decorated just as before and I realise it's almost three years to the date that we were first here. 'Get yourselves in the warm, the fire is on and I've got mulled wine on the stove and mince pies fresh out of the oven.'

I head inside, not realising that Christian and Mrs Briggs aren't with me and when I walk back to the car park, they are nowhere to be seen. I go into the room we went into on our first visit and he's already sitting there with a glass of mulled wine in his hand.

'Where did you go?' I ask, sitting down next to him.

'Just took the bags upstairs, that's all.' I'm not sure I believe him but when Mrs Briggs comes in and wishes us a Merry Christmas and then sits down, asking to be filled in on what we've been up to over the years, I forget and when Mrs Briggs shows us to our room, the bags are inside.

It isn't the little room we had before, it's far from that. There's a huge four poster bed against one wall, flowery curtains are draped around it and match the bedding and curtains at the window. There is a small table and two chairs, a large TV and after a quick look in the bathroom, there's a sunken bath and a shower.

'Oh Christian, it's perfect.' I turn to kiss him and all the anger and hurt from the past few weeks melt away and I just enjoy being back in his arms again.

Chapter 33

'Why didn't you tell me?' We're sitting on the sofa, Loose Women on the TV and enjoying a cup of tea after our romp on the stairs. In all my life, I don't think I've ever done it on the stairs, maybe up the wall, but not literally on them. And with the bruises I can feel forming on my back, I don't think it's something I will be repeating anytime soon.

'What was there to tell?' I shrug my shoulders and rest my feet on his legs. He rubs them, and I relax back in ecstasy. 'That feels nice.'

'How about telling me your mum, my mother-in-law has cancer?' He carries on with his massaging. 'I'd have come home straight away.'

'That's why I didn't tell you.' I say. 'I knew how much this meant to you and how hard it was to get messages to you anyway, if anything serious had happened, then of course I'd have told you.'

'So, being diagnosed with kidney cancer and having a kidney removed isn't serious then?' He laughs. 'Charlotte Anne Dean.' He always calls me by my maiden name when he's chiding me. 'If that's not serious, I'd hate to know what is.'

'Did the kids tell you?' I ask, knowing full well they probably did.

'I got a message through last week from them, but it was India calling head office that made me come straight home.' I nod.

'Should have known it would be India.' It's always India. She always knows exactly what I need, rather than what I think I need, and over the years she has been instrumental in many meetings that wouldn't have happened without her meddling.

'And anyway, it doesn't matter how much it meant to me. You and the kids are my priorities, always have been, always will be.' I look at the photo on the fireplace. It's of the four of us in Disneyland when the kids were ten and eight. It's one of our favourite holidays and we wish we could have visited again, but there was never quite enough money to stretch to Florida. It's not called a once in a lifetime holiday for nothing.

He's even more tanned now than in that photo, but the hair is so much greyer, perhaps the sun has lightened it even more. He's been helping bring water to villages in Africa, something he's wanted to do for years. We talked about it many times, but with the kids being little he didn't want to miss them growing up. Then when an opportunity came along that he couldn't refuse, his job allowed him a six-month hiatus and with the kids all grown up, I urged him to take it. That's why the kids and I booked a holiday to Majorca.

'You couldn't have done anything, anyway.' This is the truth. 'It's just been a waiting game.'

'I could have been there for you.' He says simply, and I wish now that I'd told him, that I'd had him at home or even on the end of the phone. I always try to be strong, independent, but sometimes you just need a shoulder to cry on or someone to rant and rave at.

Don't get me wrong, I could happily murder him sometimes when he's snoring. I've often considered holding the pillow over his face at four am when it sounds like I'm sleeping next to the Hogwarts Express. His complete inability to use the washing machine or check the contents of said washing machine to see if anything needs hanging out is another bug bear. No one in the house seems capable of emptying a bin or taking the recycling out and let's not get started on walking past the stuff on the stairs that needs to go up the stairs, hence why it's on the stairs in the bloody first place.

But overall, he's a good un. He's not perfect, of course he's not, nobody is. I know I'm not, I'm far from it. I'm messy and moody, usually because of hormone imbalances but moody none the less. I'm loud and obstinate and sulk when I don't get my own way, but if you love someone, you love their faults too, it's as simple as that. You can't change someone, and you shouldn't want to. It's what makes them, them. My assumption that everyone in the house knows that I want or need something doing has been my downfall. 'He should know, though.' Is a sentence I've quite often said or typed with Lyn's pragmatic response of, but how? If you don't ask, how does anyone know?' And now I ask, simple and effective.

'You're here now.' I move to snuggle into him, and he puts an arm around me, and we just sit there, not talking, just being, and it's the most peaceful I've felt in a long while.

'Come on you.' He stands up and then outstretches a hand to pull me up. 'Get your glad rags on and we'll grab a late lunch before visiting time.'

'But what about the kids?' I ask. 'They'll want their tea when they get in.'

'The kids are bloody twenty and twenty-two and if they can't make themselves something to eat at their age, then God help them.' I know what he's saying is true, but I like to know they've got a proper meal to come home to and he can see this on my face. 'I'll pop down the Co-op and grab them a pizza each while you get dressed.' He shakes his head. 'Honestly, we can't even go out for a meal spontaneously.' This is another of my quibbles, I am not spontaneous in the least. I don't like surprises, although I love surprising other people. I have to have everything planned to the last tiny detail and if a plan goes off schedule, well, that's it, I just throw a tantrum.

'Thank you.' I peck him on the cheek and run upstairs, jump into the shower quickly, thankful that I cut my hair off all those years ago, pop my contact lenses in, I can't see a thing without them now and don't get me started on the number of floaters I have. A quick look in the mirror and a shake of the head as to when I got old and fat, but nothing to be done about that now. It's still warm and muggy, even though we're into September, so I opt for a floaty wraparound dress, white leggings underneath to stop the chaffing thighs and slip-on shoes. I don't do sandals, got a real thing about toes. Urgh! Vile ugly things.

By the time I get down the stairs, he's already in his car waiting for me, so I scribble a note to the children, grab my bag and jump in the passenger seat.

'New dress?' He asks and I nod. 'Looks really nice.' And I can see in his eyes what he's thinking, and it makes me go all silly like a frustrated teenager. 'We could always skip lunch?' He winks at me, running a hand up my thigh.

'You promised to feed me.' As much as I'd love to run back inside with him, time is a ticking, and the kids will be home soon, and kids are the biggest passion killer ever.

'I did, didn't I.' He reverses off the drive with a sigh. 'Me and my big mouth.'

'Mum's house is empty.' I say suggestively and I notice him perk up. 'We could go there after visiting.'

'Sounds like a date to me.' He turns right at the end of our road and heads off to The Marina in Hinckley. We eat outside by the canal, watching the ducks and the boats go by. 'We still haven't had that boating holiday, have we?' He says and I shake my head.

'The kids never wanted to do it.' I reply.

'Then it's about time we started doing things for ourselves, isn't it?' The waiter places two mixed grills in front of us and I realise that I am absolutely famished.

'Speaking of which,' I really should tell him about my book.

'That's brilliant.' He beams from ear to ear. 'I'm so proud of you. Can I read it?'

'Of course you can.' I didn't think he'd want to; he doesn't really read except for the news and movie reviews on his phone. He used to when he was younger, but I think he feels it's a little childish now. I on the other hand, still love a good book. It's strange what we grow out of or stop or start doing because of what we feel we should. 'Joey's read it.' Shit, I shouldn't have just blurted that out.

'Who the hell is Joey?' His fork falls to his plate rather loudly.

'He's Mum's surgeon.'

'And you're on first name terms with him?' I can see how angry he's getting and although I know it's totally irrational, I can understand where he's coming from.

'Funny story.' I begin, but he isn't laughing. 'Do you remember me telling you about Joey Martin?'

He thinks for a minute. 'Your first kiss Joey?' He pulls that face, you know the one, where someone is saying something that can't possibly be true, but you know it is.

'The very same.' I take a bite of my sausage, trying to pretend this conversation is perfectly normal and your first love ends up as your mum's surgeon all the time. It sounds like something from Jerry Springer. *My first kiss was with my mum's surgeon, tell all exclusive.*

I giggle to myself at this, but he's not laughing.

'And how, pray tell, has he read your book?' His face is like thunder.

'Oh my God.' I look at him. 'You're jealous.'

'I am not.' He pops a chip into his mouth as if to emphasise the point.

'As if anyone would look twice at me.'

'Don't start putting yourself down again.' Another of my bad traits is always, always looking down at myself. 'You are gorgeous, inside and out, and Joey bloody Martin would be lucky to have you.'

'Well Joey bloody Martin can't have me.' I kiss him over the table. 'And neither can anyone else for that matter, except maybe Jonathan Bailey, but then he wouldn't want me because you know, obvious reasons, then there's David Tenant, oh and Matt Smith, have you seen him as Dameon Targaryen? No of course you haven't, Orlando Bloom…'

'Ok, I get it.' At least he's laughing again. 'Unless one of your celebrity crushes comes along.'

'Not even then, because I am, one hundred percent yours.' I kiss him again. 'Ok, maybe Rege Jēan Page dressed in his Bridgerton outfit.'

We drop his car back home and pop in briefly to see the children before grabbing mine and heading to the hospital. The parking pass has proved invaluable over the years. Ok, it's a little walk from work to the hospital but saves a fortune.

He opens the glove box.

'You didn't open my present.' He pulls out a small red box tied with a bow.

'I didn't know it was there.'

'You mean to tell me that you haven't been in your glove box for three months?'

'Haven't needed to.' I shrug. 'There's only the key for my wheel nuts and the car manual in there. I moved my CDs into the boot ages ago.'

'I got you something.' He pulls on the bow and opens the box. 'Just like last time.'

Chapter 34

'Morning Sleepy Head.' Christian walks in carrying a tray and places it on the table that stands in the bay window of the room. It must have been the attic of the house because it has low beams and a sloping roof, but it's obviously on the same side as the single room we had last time because it looks out onto the sea. 'I've got toast and cereal and a fresh pot of tea.' He sneaks onto the bed. 'We missed the fry up again.' He says, winking at me cheekily. 'One day we might actually get to try Mrs Briggs' breakfast.'

It's like we can't get enough of each other when we're alone. Even though we've been together for over three years now, because two of those years he's been at university, it still feels so fresh and new. I stretch out on the bed, and as I do, the cover slips down.

The toast and tea are cold by the time we get round to them, so Christian makes a fresh pot with the kettle and tea bags in the room and we sit at the table like proper grown-ups.

'You remembered.' I look down at my bowl of muesli to find every single offensive raisin has been removed.

'Of course.' He smiles at me over his bowl of Frosties. 'So, I've got a little secret.' I eye him suspiciously. 'We're here for a few nights.' He holds his hand up to stop me from talking. 'Before you say anything, it is all arranged. Your mum called work and booked you Monday to Wednesday off. My university and your college are all finished for the term so we can have a proper little holiday, just you and me.'

'My mum knows we're staying in a room together?' He shook his head.

'I told a little lie and said we'd have separate rooms. I'm not sure she believed me, but you know, what can she do.' He looks at me so innocently, but with such a devilish look behind his eyes. 'I've booked us a restaurant for tonight and I thought we could take a moonlight walk like last time. We can explore the area in the day, I think there's a castle nearby and by night...' He trails off and raises his eyebrows suggestively. 'We can make up for lost time.'

'Well, that's your fault the lost time.' I say, bristling a little when I remember. 'I'm not sure I've quite forgiven you yet.'

'You will.' He gobbles down his cereal. 'When you see what Susie and I have been working on.' I can't help it put I pause in my eating, and he notices. 'There is nothing going on with me and Susie.'

'I bet she'd like there to be, though.'

'I doubt it.'

'What do you mean by that?'

'Put it this way.' He explains. 'I don't think I'm her type.' I look at him, unable to follow a word he's saying. 'You're more her type if you get my meaning.'

'Eh?' Then light dawns. 'Oh.' I say. 'But she's slept with all the guys in the house.

'Think she's been working through some issues.' He pours us both a cup of tea. 'She thought she might be bi, so has been experimenting a bit but she's decided, after Ryan, that she's definitely one hundred percent a lesbian.'

'Well, Ryan's enough to turn anyone into a lesbian.' I say, laughing.

Christian joins in. 'He's a good lad really, just not too confident with the ladies.'

'Not too confident with the ladies.' I spit my tea out. 'Here love, hold me pint while I scratch my knob and ogle your boobs. Don't mind if I cop a feel do ya?' I say this in a mock northern accent.

'Ok, so he needs some practise.' Christian shrugs helplessly.

'He needs more than practise; he needs a whole personality transplant.'

'Hey, that's my best mate you're talking about.'

'I'm right though, aren't I?'

'He'll find someone, don't you worry.' He sits back in the chair and looks out of the window. 'There's someone for everyone.'

'There is indeed. I mean, just look at you.' He gives me a look through slanted eyes.

'Ha ha, very funny, my sides are splitting.'

'You know I'm only teasing.' I stand up and walk round to his side of the table. 'I think you're perfect.' I kneel and undo his trousers. He's ready instantly, and it's another hour before we finally get outside.

The restaurant is packed when we arrive, office Christmas parties are in full swing, and the odd couple dotted here and there adds to a lively atmosphere. The waiter shows us to a table in the corner by the open fireplace and we place our coats on the back of our chairs. Christian keeps tapping his trouser pocket, I'm not sure why. Perhaps he's checking he's got his wallet or something.

We order burgers. It's funny how we always order the same thing, even with desserts. We then laugh and sing along with the music and the disco that has just started. There's people up dancing already and it's so lovely to see everyone having a good time.

'Christmas is just brilliant, isn't it?' I say to Christian, having to shout to make myself heard over the noise.

The opening bars of a song by Donna Lewis blast out. 'Shall we dance?' He holds out his hand and leads me to the dance floor and proceeds to sing the chorus to me. 'I love you, always, forever.'

Just as the song fades, the DJ picks up his microphone.

'Good evening, ladies and gentlemen. I hope we're all having a good time.' There are cheers and whistles. 'I've just got to halt the music for a moment because someone's got something special they want to ask someone special.'

I look round the room, expecting the staff to come out with a birthday cake, but instead I find Christian down on one knee in front of me. He has an open jewellery box in his hand and a ring inside. The room has gone incredibly silent with the odd 'Oh!' from female guests who have just realised what's happening and a good natured 'Go on my son' from a drunk gentleman at the bar.

'Charlotte Anne Dean.' He says, not once taking his eyes off mine. 'Will you marry me?'

'Yes!' I say without hesitation. 'A hundred times, yes.' Everyone cheers and claps, the DJ plays Congratulations by Cliff Richard and after Christian has placed the ring on my finger, we are treated to handshakes and slaps on the back from well-wishers. We go back to the table and the manager brings out a bottle of champagne. 'How did you know my size?' I can't stop looking at the ring. It's a diamond solitaire, encased in gold and fits me to perfection.

'The girls took one of yours from your room.'

'My dragon one, by any chance?' He nodded. 'I wondered why it had disappeared and magically reappeared two weeks later. So, they all know?'

He nods. 'They do.'

'Little gits.' I look across to the disco. 'And the DJ?'

'Him too, I asked him to play our song.'

'Our song? I didn't know we had a song.'

'We do now.' And he hums the chorus again.

'I'm going to have to watch you Mr Sawyer, you're far too good at keeping secrets.'

We walk back to Mistletoe Inn, taking the extra-long walk along the beach while the tide is out. It's like going back three years to the first time we made love and the first time I really, genuinely knew that we loved each other. Not just because of the sex, although that helped, but because I felt and still feel, truly connected to him and now we're engaged and he's mine and I'm his, always, forever.

It will be years before we can even think about getting married. He's still at university and it's years before I'll be a fully qualified accountant. I'm not even sure I want to be anymore. I've passed my AAT, just, I had to re-do the tax exam, but I'm not sure an accounts office is for me. I hate the office politics, the back biting, and the bitchy comments. The work is the same over and over, just a different client each day, or week. There's a little bit of respite when we go out on audit. We were taken to a lovely farm over the summer and were treated like royalty, but sometimes you're just shoved in a dingy room and treated like the enemy. I honestly don't know what people have against accountants. We're only doing our job after all.

We're sitting on the wall at the back of the hotel, looking out at the sea and the moon and how bright the stars are.

'Will you marry me?' He asks again, taking my hand.

'I've already said yes, you daft wally.' I slap him playfully.

'I don't mean in the future.' He jumps onto the sand and stands in front of me. 'I mean now.'

'How can we get married now?' I say. 'It's almost midnight.'

'Well, not now exactly.' He runs his hand through his hair in his nervous way.

'I don't know what you mean, Christian.' I'm very confused. He's asked me to marry him, I've said yes, no doubt whatsoever that I want to marry him, but he's babbling on about getting married now. 'It takes ages to plan a wedding and we haven't got any money to pay for one either.' When Lyn's sister got married, it cost nearly ten thousand pounds. I've got about three hundred in my savings.

'Will you marry me?' He asks again. 'Tomorrow?' And he pulls out a letter in an envelope addressed to him. 'Read it.' There's a lamppost in Mrs Brigg's back garden, it reminds me of the one from Narnia, black, ornate and old-fashioned. It's currently festooned with fairy lights as well, so I walk up to it and unfold the letter. Christian is silent the whole time. 'This is what I've been planning.'

The letter is on Basildon Bond paper, you know, the really posh stuff where you have a sheet with lines on it you shove underneath, so it looks like you can write in straight lines without actually writing on straight lines.

Dear Mr Sawyer,

Thank you for your letters and phone calls. I have conversed with Mavis Briggs and Arnold Porter and after careful consideration I would be delighted to marry you and Miss

Dean on Monday the 9th of December at two pm. I will arrange the necessary reading of the Banns which you will need to attend and look forward to welcoming you to our church.

Yours sincerely

Reverend Kemp

St Barbara in the field.

'But that's tomorrow.' I'm lost for words, not something that happens very often, but I am totally and utterly lost for words.

'So how about it?' he asks. 'Fancy becoming Mrs Sawyer?'

Chapter 35

'So?' I wake up to find Christian hovering over me like an eager child on Christmas morning.

'You're really serious, aren't you?' I hoist myself up in the bed and lean on the headboard and he sits in front of me cross-legged. 'It's not a prank, a little joke or something?' He shakes his head.

'I am deadly serious.'

'But why?' I don't understand the hurry, or how he expects to pull off a wedding, or how we'd live together afterwards.

'Because I want to be married to you. I want to wake up every day and see your face and go to bed every night the same way.' He makes it sound so romantic, but I don't think he's thought any of this through.

'I want the same Christian, but I can't give up my job and move in with you in your student house and you can't give up your degree.' I take hold of his hand. 'We don't have any money to buy a house. The last of your savings went on fixing the Capri and I've got three hundred pounds.'

'I'll sell my car.' He says, and now I know he's serious. He loves that car, sometimes more than he loves me.

'You don't need to sell your car.'

'I'll quit university, sell the car and get a job in Coventry.'

'Right, stop there.' I put my hand up. 'I love you more than anything in the whole world and I want nothing more than to be your wife one day in the future, but Christian, think about it.'

I can see I'm getting through to him at last, but the happiness in his face is draining by the second and I feel so sad to be doing this to him.

'What if we just got married?' I sigh in exasperation. 'And didn't tell anyone?'

'How can we not tell anyone?' Has he gone completely bonkers? 'We'll be married, husband and wife. I'll be Mrs Sawyer.'

'But only we'd know.' I scrunch my face up in thought. 'Even if you're married, you only change your name because you start using it and tell banks and people like that. You can still be Miss Dean, but you and I would know that really, you're Mrs Sawyer.' He's smiling at me now, quite possibly the biggest smile I've ever seen.

'Er…' I honestly can't think of anything to say again.

'Think about it?' I've been doing nothing but think about it since last night. 'You and I get married today, carry on as normal. How utterly romantic is that?'

'You said you wanted to be married so you could wake up beside me and go to sleep next to me every day.' I'm not convinced. 'We'd be no different from what we are now.'

'We'd be married.' He says this as if it's the easiest thing in the world.

'What about our family and friends? They'd want to be here.' Well, my mum would probably try and stop it, *you're far too young* she would say, even though she was nineteen when she married my dad, but when you say things like that, all you get is, *it was different in our day.*

'We can do it again in a few years when we've got the money and the house and stuff.' He throws himself on the bed and lies down next to me, taking my left hand in his. 'I don't want to wait years and years to be married to you. I asked you to marry me because I want to be married to you, not engaged to you.'

'Have you really booked a church?' He nods.

'And I've been three times on a Sunday to hear the Banns being read.'

'You've travelled up here three times?' He nods again.

'That's why I couldn't come back to Coventry.' He kisses the ring on my finger. 'Say you'll marry me?' He asks again and I'm starting to waver. I mean what harm is there in it, really? We just stand in the church and say a few words and then we're married, we love each other, we're going to do it one day anyway, why not today?

'And we don't tell anyone?' This sounds very appealing; I really don't think I could tell my mum this. I wish I could. I wish we had the kind of relationship where I could tell her anything without fear of being shouted at or judged. And I know if I were in trouble, real, serious trouble, she would be there, probably with a stern word afterwards, but she would be there.

Like when Christian and I came back from our first weekend here, I swear to God she could tell we'd lied to her, or she'd know we'd had sex, of course she couldn't and technically we didn't lie to her. Still, I felt bad and walked on eggshells for weeks just in case I slipped up.

'We don't tell anyone.' He puts a finger on his lips. 'Obviously, Mrs Briggs and Arnold know.'

'Ok.'

'And Susie knows.' He looks at me sheepishly. 'I told you she'd been helping me.'

'India? She usually does.' He shakes his head.

'No, I've kept it a secret from them, too.' He pauses for a second. 'And I told Ryan.'

'I just don't know Christian.' One minute I think yes, then my brain clicks in again. 'I haven't even got a dress.' I know the contents of my suitcase contain nothing more glamourous than jeans and a slightly dressy shirt. 'I can't get married in any old rubbish, can I?'

'Well now, you see, that's where Susie comes in.' He dashes out of the room and comes back in a few moments later carrying one of those hanger bags that posh frocks and suits go in, so you don't crease them.

'Christian?' I know exactly what is going to be in there and I think it might be one step too far. 'Is that why Susie was questioning me about wedding dresses when I last came up?' I had thought it was odd at the time.

'She wasn't very subtle, was she?' He says. 'Now, I'm just going to put it here for you and then I'm going to make myself scarce and either way, I'm happy with whatever you decide.' He hangs the dress on the wardrobe door and then crawls over the bed to kiss me. 'I love you Charlie, from the first moment I saw you and I want to be your husband, even if it's just our secret for now. Nothing would make me prouder than to call you my wife. But if you don't want that yet, I understand that too and we'll just go back to how we were, and it won't make a blind bit of difference.' He kisses me again and then heads to the door.

'I love you, Christian.' I say as he walks through, still unsure of what my decision will actually be.

'Always, forever Charlie.'

Chapter 36

We're a solemn group that leave the hospital that Friday afternoon.

'Mum took it well I thought.' Rob says, and we all agree.

'She did.' I say. 'I think it's us that didn't.'

'It's not too bad though, is it?' Rob's wife says. 'I mean it's not brilliant, dance on the ceiling kind of news but it's ok, it's manageable.'

'And they said they'd found this bit early.' Always look on the bright side of life.

'A few rounds of chemo should sort it.' He'd said. We hadn't seen Joey. Why would we? He was the surgeon, this time it was Mum's consultant. He'd explained to us that it had spread a little further than they had first thought, but with treatment it should shrink. They weren't able to remove as much as they'd wanted, some vital wotsit or other, but Mum seemed ok with the news. I just think she was glad to finally sleep without having to go to the toilet every hour.

'They said she's making excellent progress too and can come home on Monday.' Mum's face lit up at those words. 'The kids are dying to see her.'

'We're not telling Nan, are we?' Rob asks, and I shake my head.

'Mum doesn't want anyone else knowing at the moment. She said she had enough of sympathetic looks the first time.'

'You parked outside of work?' Rob asks and I nod. 'We're over there.' He points to the main car park, and we part ways at the revolving doors after hugs and kisses all round.

'How are you really, though?' He asks when we get back in the car.

'Honestly?' I turn to face him. 'I don't know. I knew it was coming after Joey told me but like before, it hits you when you're sitting there in that room and they tell you.'

'Your mum is such a strong woman, though.' He pulls me in for a hug because he can see I'm on the verge of tears.

'I know, it's just after all that with Dad and almost losing Nan last October and Mum breaking her ankle, she was just starting to enjoy herself again and go on holiday with her friend and trips to London.'

'And she'll do all that again soon.' He wipes my tears away with his thumb. 'We just need to get her through this first. And we will.' He smiles at me, and I look up at him, at a face I've known for almost thirty years. Eyes that have searched my soul a million times in those years, eyes with tiny crinkles in the corner now and hair that is greyer than brown.

I have no doubt that he loves me, has always loved me, has been there for me through all the good times and the bad, just as I have for him. Through grief and heartache and tremendous joys. That no matter what, he will be there for me for thirty more years to come and more, God willing.

'Home?' I ask, turning the key.

'Home.' He says, popping in the CD he made me before he went away with the words *Till I'm Home Again* written on the disc.

The opening bars of our song begin.

'I love you, Christian.'

'Always, forever Charlie.'

Chapter 37

December the 9th 2026

'Are you nervous?' My daughter asks me, as she adds the finishing touches to my makeup as we sit in front of the mirror in the bedroom.

'It sounds silly, but I am.' She holds her hands on my shoulders and smiles at me from behind.

'You look beautiful, Mum.' I squeeze her hands with mine and stand up.

'Are we ready, then?' She helps me take off the robe that has been covering my dress and then she takes a step back.

'Its gorgeous Mum.' I twirl round gently, the soft folds of the deep red dress rustle slightly and the gold embroidery shimmers in the light. The dress is cut low over my bust. You got to make use of what you've got and then flows out in an A-line to skim my bum and stomach. Three-quarter sleeves are there, because you know, it's winter, but really, they cover my bingo wings.

My son knocks on the door, ready to escort me, and my new son-in-law takes my daughter's arm.

She looks stunning. She's wearing the dress that hung up in this very room, thirty years ago today. We've changed it and altered it to fit her. I've never been a size ten and we dyed it red to match my dress with a gold sash. My son and son-in-law are in black suits with red shirts and yellow carnations.

'I wish Grandad was here to see this.' My son kisses me before offering me his arm.

It's my only regret today. That my dad isn't here to walk me down the aisle, that he never got to walk me down the aisle.

A black Ford Capri waits in the driveway of Mistletoe Inn and neighbours line the street on the way to St Barbara's in the field. We've lived here for just over a year now. It's been a mad few years. My book, Meet Me at Our Spot, after several rejections, was picked up and released in the spring of 2024 and after we learnt that Mrs Briggs was retiring, we put an offer in which she accepted without hesitation.

Neither of us knew how to run a Bed & Breakfast but with Mrs Briggs and Arnold's help, we muddled our way through, and it gives us time together to enjoy our lives more and I've started writing another book as well. We always leave the little room free for any waifs and strays that may need it one day.

The church is beautiful, it's on a slight cliff overlooking the sea and after a cold spell last night, it's covered in frost still and glistens as we walk through the graveyard. The girls are there at the door and faff with my dress before going inside.

'Ready?' My son looks at me and takes my arm.

'Ready.' The opening bars of I love you, always, forever ring out in a slower version. It seemed an appropriate song to walk down the aisle to after he'd proposed to it all those years ago. We never did get around to the big wedding. We had our secret one and then when we moved in together, we told people we were already married. It was easier then, changing passports and bank details with a change of address.

Mum wasn't happy, of course she wasn't but by some miracle, Rob's first child was born that day and it was all forgotten in a blur of first grandchild and she even threw us a surprise fifth anniversary party along with Christian's mum.

Then the kids came along and then we never seemed to have the time or the money and then Dad got ill, and it was just one excuse after another so a few months ago, I asked Christian to marry me on the back wall of the garden under the Narnia lamppost. And of course, he said yes.

He has his back to me as I enter the church. Even from this angle, he's handsome. His best man, Ryan, gives me a cheeky wink before turning back to face the front. There's Susie and her wife. I've always liked Susie. Ryan's wife is next to them. She's twenty years younger than him and pregnant with their first baby, we always joke about why he couldn't find the right girl, because she hadn't been born yet.

There's Mrs Briggs who is actually now Mrs Porter after she and Arnold got married in 2010, but we still call her Mrs Briggs and Arnold of course, smiling at me. Some friends from work have made the trip and Christian's mum and dad stand proudly on the front row and on the right and to the left, there's my mum and Rob and sister-in-law. I can see Mum has been crying already.

We had another trip to the doctor last month. It's a quarterly occurrence now, but it's no better and no worse so now she's living with cancer rather than dying from it. She moved here with us after we lost Nan at the ripe old age of one hundred and two. Then finally, when I'm just a few steps away, he turns.

Whether it's the surroundings, or just the nature of the day but I'm transported back to 1996 when I stood at this very place and pledged my life to him at the age of twenty. He's smiling as he takes my hand from our son's and he pecks me on the cheek, whispering that he loves me as he does.

We've written our own vows; we didn't have a chance to the last time. It was so hurried that day. I only decided to go through with it at half-past one and Mrs Briggs had to help me into the dress and drive me to the church. The dress Susie had chosen for me was almost perfect, a little tight and not quite the style I would have chosen for myself, but at least I had a wedding dress.

Christian was coming out of the church as I arrived, and I'll never forget the look on his face. The realisation that I was there at that moment in the wedding dress made him almost collapse and Arnold, who was our other witness, had to help him off the floor.

But today is different, today has been planned.

'Christian, when you came into my life, I didn't know the impact that you would have on me. You lift me up when I'm down, make me happy when I'm sad and I couldn't imagine a day without you in my life.'

'Charlie, thirty years ago today, we stood here and became husband and wife. The invisible girl that deserves to stand in the spotlight every day. Not a day goes by when I don't thank my lucky stars that you agreed to marry me that day.'

It's a short ceremony followed by a meal at the pub Christian proposed in all those years ago, then after changing and leaving Mr and Mrs Porter in charge of Mistletoe Inn for two weeks we head off in the Capri, feeling like two teenagers again. Much like 1996, I have absolutely no idea where we're going and eventually, we pull up to a marina.

'A canal boat?' I ask.

'It's what we said we always wanted to do.' He grabs the suitcase out of the car, throws the key to our son who has followed us there with Rob. 'Look after her.' He warns because you know, it's his absolute pride and joy and only comes out of the garage on special occasions.

'But in the winter?' He looks at me, puts the case on the floor, and takes my hands in his.

'Just think of all the things we can do to keep warm.' He winks at me before kissing me and that old familiar feeling floods my insides.

'Urgh! Get a room.' Our son says before revving the Capri and wheel spinning away.

'That boy!' Christian scolds, laughing at the same time. 'This way.'

He leads me into a small building where we pick up the keys and a manual and get a quick tour of the boat and how it works etc…then we are on our way.

'We should have done this years ago.' I say. It's bloody freezing but we're wrapped up against the cold, Christian on the tiller with nothing but countryside around us and a cup of hot chocolate in our hands.

'I love you, Mrs Sawyer.'

'Always, forever Mr Sawyer.'

THE END

A Little Note

First, a huge thank you for reading and I hope that you enjoyed the story as much as I enjoyed writing it. This story came to me at a hard time in my life when my own mother was diagnosed with kidney cancer and it helped me to process all the feelings that this entailed.

Some of the experiences of Charlie are my own experiences and some are completely fictional. We did lose my dad to dementia and not a day goes by that I don't miss him.

I want to say thank you to my mum for the love and support she gives to me; I honestly couldn't ask for a better mum.

To my oldest friends, I don't know where I would be without you.

Thank you to all my author friends who support me and help me and a specially thank you to Kim for her time and patience when I'm bouncing cover ideas off her.

Once again, a huge thank you to Anita Faulkner and the Chick Lit and Prosecco group on Facebook for their tireless support.

Sue Baker, you are just wonderful.

Thank you to Kelly at Celtic Edits for helping me knock this book into shape and Amanda at Lets Get Booked for turning my cover into a beautiful paperback.

To Jane, you are amazing.

About the Author

I was born in Coventry but now live in Nuneaton. I married the love of my life over 20 years ago and we have two almost grown-up children. We share our lives with two mad dogs as well.

Writing is a great passion of mine. I love creating stories and characters, they help me escape from the world for a while and I hope readers feel the same.

I am a huge fan of All Creatures Great and Small, Call the Midwife and Bridgerton. I love history and romance.

I also write for children as Lily Mae Walters.

Coming Soon

Look out for my autumnal romance with a sprinkling of spice on September 5th, 2023.

By Florence Keeling

A Little in Love

The Word is Love

Please Remember Me

Love, Lies and Family Ties

By Lily Mae Walters

Josie James and The Teardrops of Summer

Josie James and The Velvet Knight

Brittle's Academy for The Magically Unstable

Follow me on Twitter

@CharlieADean

@KeelingFlorence

@LilyMaeWalters1

Printed in Great Britain
by Amazon

23787025R00155